PAPER CRAFT
school

READER'S
DIGEST
Learn-As-You-Go-Guide

PAPER
CRAFT
school

CLIVE STEVENS

Reader's
Digest

THE READER'S DIGEST ASSOCIATION, INC.
Pleasantville New York Montreal

A READER'S DIGEST BOOK

Designed and edited by Quarto Publishing plc

Senior Art Editor *Penny Cobb*
Senior Editors *Sian Parkhouse, Sally MacEachern*
Text Editor *Mary Senechal*
Designer *Sheila Volpe*
Picture Researcher *Susannah Jayes*
Picture Manager *Giulia Hetherington*
Photographers *Laura Wickenden, Paul Forrester*
Illustrations *Dave Kemp*
Editorial Director *Mark Dartford*
Art Director *Moira Clinch*

The credits that appear on page 176 are hereby made a part of
this copyright page

Library of Congress Cataloging in Publication Data

Stevens, Clive.
     Papercraft school / Clive Stevens.
          p.   cm.—(Reader's digest learn-as-you-go guide)
     ISBN 0-89577-873-4
     1. Paper work.   I. Title.   II. Series.
  TT870.S73   1996
  745.54–dc20   96–11754

Reader's Digest and the Pegasus logo are registered trademarks
of The Reader's Digest Association, Inc.

Printed in Singapore

Foreword

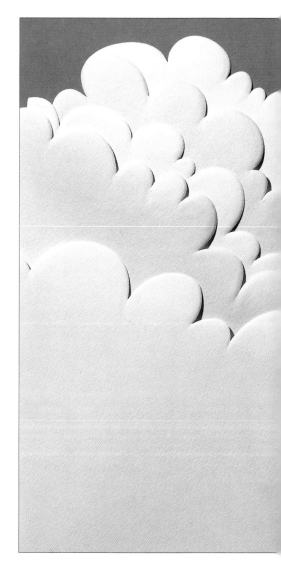

At some time in their lives everyone has used paper as an art medium: to draw and paint on, to make a collage, to construct three-dimensional forms from cut-out shapes or papier mâché. In fact, paper is probably the most versatile art material there is. There are so many different art forms based on paper that we could not include them all in this book. Rather, we concentrate on those that use the paper itself as the medium, from simple weaving and collage to more ambitious art forms, such as advanced pop-ups and paper sculpture. All of the basic techniques are straightforward and easy to accomplish. By trying the projects in order you will be guided through a series of achievements that increase in complexity as you proceed, leaving you with all the skills necessary to create your own original paper masterpieces.

Working with paper can be very absorbing, and it is an ideal medium for all ages. Paper is readily available and inexpensive, and paper crafts need little special equipment.

As you proceed through the book, pay special attention to the details in the exciting works of the artists featured on the gallery pages and discover their wonderful techniques. By trying these you will find your own individual style.

Clive Stevens

Contents

Introduction

INTRODUCTION

Paper is a material that most of us take for granted today. We use it to record the world's knowledge, print the morning news, write financial transactions, wrap food, and decorate our homes, to name but a few of its many applications. Attributed to the Chinese, paper was invented during the Han dynasty (202 B.C. to A.D. 220). But the art of papermaking remained a closely guarded secret for almost 500 years, and its spread throughout the rest of the world was very slow. It was not until the seventh century that it was introduced into Japan through Korea, at about the same time as Buddhism.

Originally, paper had an important role in religion, utilized for its symbolic purity and for the distribution of holy texts. Gradually, it began to be used for practical purposes, such as floor coverings and sail cloths, sliding screens, masks, kites, and even clothing.

It was the Arabs who took paper to the rest of the world. Having captured the secret of paper making along with the Chinese prisoners they took during an attack on the city of Samarkand in A.D. 751, they developed their own manufacturing sites, and began exporting paper to Europe. By the fifteenth century, production was widespread throughout Europe, and paper had replaced papyrus, parchment, and vellum as a writing material. In 1690, the first paper mill was established in North America.

ORIGAMI AND PAPERCUTS

From very early in its history paper was exploited for its aesthetic as well as for its functional qualities. Used by artists as a surface on which to produce art, it was also a medium in its own right. One of the most familiar and instantly recognizable forms of paper arts is origami. It is a matter of dispute whether origami originated in Japan, Korea, or China, but we do know that the Japanese were producing sophisticated forms

NEWSPRINT

Newspapers are generally made from cheap, poor-quality pulp with a high acid content. Newsprint differs in color and tends to turn brown over time.

HANDMADE PAPER PRODUCTION

This photograph of Whatman's famous Springfield Paper Mill, taken circa 1905, shows the former dipping the mold and deckle in the vat and the coucher waiting behind the pile of blankets, ready to couch the freshly formed sheet.

some 1,200 years ago. The word itself is Japanese, from *ori* (to fold) and *kami* (paper). The popularity of the art died out until the 1930s, when a young Japanese man called Akira Yoshizawa began developing new forms based on old designs. Unlike the traditional form of origami, which allowed the paper to be cut as well as folded, the newer forms kept to strict rules that demanded that all shapes should be created from a single piece of paper using folds only. The popularity of origami spread to the West and was confirmed by the publication in 1956 of a British book called *Paper Magic* by the South African, Robert Harbin, and later books by an American, Samuel Randlett.

Some of the earliest forms of paper art are Chinese paper cuts dating from the twelfth century A.D. These were used to adorn paper-covered windows. Polish paper cuts date from around the same time. Traditionally made by peasant women, they were used to decorate the home. Different techniques were specific to different regions, so that the source of a design could be identified by whether it was created using two folds, which produced four identical squares, or one fold, which created bilateral symmetry. Paper cutting also had a tradition in many other

ORIGINS OF ORIGAMI
Origami in Japan dates back 1,200 years. This eighteenth century painting shows the courtesan Segawa of the Ogiya (house) holding a paper crane – a classic origami design. (Utamaro, from the series "Yukun Waka Sannin").

MODERN PAPERCUT
This amazingly intricate papercut is based on a well-known Chinese literary classic. The artist used Chinese calligraphy paper, a craft knife, and a pointed pair of Chinese scissors (collection of David Chu).

parts of the world, particularly the Netherlands, and areas of the United States with a strong Dutch influence, such as Pennsylvania. The subject matter often included pastoral scenes and family groups.

PAPER SCULPTURE AND POP-UPS

It is believed that modern paper sculpture originated in Poland. After seeing the works of Polish artists in Continental exhibitions, English and American artists became influenced by it. Many Polish artists emigrated to America taking their talents with them. In the 1940s and 1950s big department stores seized on paper sculpture as a versatile and exciting new means of creating window displays that were relatively quick to construct, had an architectural effect, and were inexpensive. Advertising agencies, too, were quick to recognize the appeal and effectiveness of paper sculpture, and it was used in numerous campaigns. Although its popularity died down, there was renewed interest in the 1970s. Today it is an enormously popular art form.

Another paper art form that has been exploited by the advertising and graphic arts industry is pop-ups. A specialized form of paper sculpture, pop-ups were first used in children's books during the latter half of the nineteenth century. They were very expensive to produce, however, and so they declined in popularity until the 1950s, when much innovative work was done

HISTORICAL PAPERCUT
This fine papercut was executed with a sharp knife. Note how the artist achieved intricate petal detail using a series of delicate cut-outs (collection of Nancy Rosin).

DECOUPAGE
This attractive perfume box is a typical example of nineteenth century decoupage. The many layers of varnish give it a lacquered finish.

10

in Czechoslovakia. American and British publishers were inspired to create their own books, and with the development of more sophisticated printing techniques, costs were lowered sufficiently for pop-ups to be produced on a large scale. It was not long before greeting card manufacturers began to use pop-ups, and the medium was explored and developed to create the huge variety of complex and ingenious designs available.

Today, paper artists have even more to inspire them. They can draw on traditional and historical techniques, like those described in this book, and either practice them in their purest forms, or adapt them bringing modern design values and style to their work. And never before has there been a greater range of paper types, weights, colors, and textures available, as you can see in the "Directory of Papers" on pages 16 to 21. Paper is an inspiration in itself, to be admired for its own innate beauty, and also a medium for creating stunning works of art.

POP-UP ADVERTISEMENT
This fine example of a magic box mechanism dates from circa 1910. As the card is opened the teacups and loaf of bread rise up from the table (Robert Opie).

POP-UP BOOK
These pop-up books from the 1930s make use of two mechanisms: a multiple layer mechanism on the left and a V-fold on the right (Robert Opie).

Materials

Paper

MATERIALS

Paper is available in a wide variety of types. The "Directory of Papers" on pages 16–21 contains specific advice on which type is best suited for the particular application you have in mind. But paper is a ubiquitous medium. We encounter it in numerous different forms every day, and it is helpful to have some knowledge about its general nature.

The papers we most commonly come into contact with are newsprint and bond. Newsprint, a low-grade paper made from mechanical pulp, or groundwood, is used for printing newspapers. Groundwood is made by grinding peeled logs in a stream of water until the wood is broken down into fibers. It is an ideal medium for papermaking and papier mâché.

Bond is made in a wide variety of qualities, the highest quality from 100 percent rag pulp, and the lower-grade stocks from greater proportions of groundwood. Bond paper is sized (sealed with a glue mixture) to prevent penetration by writing and drawing inks and is commonly used as stationery in offices. It is a versatile paper and can be used when the project you are working on does not require specific qualities.

Other common terms that you will come across when buying paper are *coated, rag, laid,* and *wove.* Coated papers have been specially treated with a surface coating to improve their printing quality. Rag papers are made from a high percentage of fiber from cotton or linen rags and so are of a very high quality. Rag papers are often used for watercolor painting. Laid and wove refer to the appearance of the paper, which results from the way in which it is produced. Laid papers have a fine pattern of parallel lines, caused by metal rods in the mold, while wove paper has an almost imperceptible mesh pattern.

SAMPLE SWATCHES
You can obtain swatch books in a variety of colors, textures, and types from paper manufacturers.

WHERE TO BUY PAPER

Art supply stores sell the biggest range of papers, card, and mat board. There is no problem with quantity – you can buy as little as one sheet. However, if you want a larger quantity of one type of paper, it may be less expensive to obtain it directly from the paper manufacturer, or from a paper wholesaler. Wholesalers will also supply you with sample swatches free of charge if you request them. These can be very useful for projects that require lots of small pieces in different colors or finishes, such as collage. Another good source for paper is local printers. They buy in quantity for specific jobs and often have paper left over that they will be happy to sell to you. Their prices will be considerably lower than at the art stores, but your choice will be limited and you will probably have to buy a minimum quantity.

PAPER WEIGHT AND SIZE

Paper is sold by weight, and different grades of the same type of paper are distinguished by how much a standard quantity of that paper actually weighs. In most of the world, that standard is a sheet of paper 1 meter square, and the weight is measured in terms of grams per square meter (expressed as g/m^2 or gsm).

In the United States, though, we express weight in pounds, and we use the system of basis weights. The standard quantity is a ream, or 500 sheets, but the size of the sheets varies from one category of paper to another. The basis size of bond paper, for example, is 17×22 inches, while the basis size of newsprint is 24×36 inches. Thus, a 50-pound bond paper is actually much heavier than a 50-pound newsprint. The papers in the "Directory of Papers" are described as light (under 70 lbs), medium (70–120 lbs), and heavy (120–200 lbs).

You need to understand both systems of measurement since you will come across both American-made and foreign papers.

Paper is available in single sheets.

You can also buy pads in different colors and sizes.

ORIGAMI PAPERS
Available in 12-in. (30 cm) and 4-in. (10 cm) squares in a range of colors; some have a different color on the back.

FANCY PAPERS
Printed pattern papers can be very effective for origami.

Directory of Papers

MATERIALS

The type, texture, weight, and color of paper affect suitability for each art form. For example, origami needs a thin paper that can be folded repeatedly without buckling; pop-ups and paper sculptures require robust papers that can stand firmly. The texture and finish of the paper are also important to the appearance of your work. Handmade papers can be hot-pressed, cold-pressed, or rough. Hot-pressed paper is fairly smooth, cold-pressed has a slight texture, or "tooth," and rough paper has a distinct texture. Other treatments, such as coatings, will also affect the surface quality of commercial papers.

Fortunately, despite the apparently complex array of choice, paper can be categorized into the four basic groups listed below:

Uncoated papers comprise the majority of machine-made papers used in the printing industry, many of which are carried by art supply stores and paper distributors. They include white and colored papers in a range of plain and embossed finishes. Their fibers align in one direction, making folding easy.

Coated papers have highly smooth surfaces on one or both sides and are available in gloss or dull finishes of various brightness. The colored papers are good for torn sculptural effects or collage, because they reveal an attractive white edge when torn.

Handmade papers are generally produced from cotton or linen rags and used by watercolor and etching artists. They are available from art supply stores and handmade paper companies. Their sculptural qualities are superb, because the fibers occur in a random pattern.

Specialty papers include crepe, tracing, and corrugated papers – in fact, all of the papers that fall outside of the other three groups.

Commercial Uncoated

SCORED

CURLED

CRUMPLED

TORN

COVER PAPER
The kind of paper used for booklets and folders. Available in white and a wide range of colors, including bright primaries. Suitable for weaving, collage, papercuts, pop-ups, papermaking, and paper sculpture. Weight: medium.

BOND PAPER
Everyday paper, available as office and home stationery. Supplied mainly in shades of white, cream, and pale gray or blue. Suitable for weaving, collage, papercuts, origami, papermaking, papier mâché, and paper sculpture. Weight: medium.

SCORED

CURLED

CRUMPLED

TORN

ART PAPER

Fine paper sold for use by artists, available in various colors. Suitable for weaving, collage, papercuts, pop-ups, papermaking, and paper sculpture. Weight: white, heavy; colors, medium.

DRAWING PAPER

A strong, more opaque bond of the kind used in sketchbooks, available in white and a range of bright and pale colors. Suitable for collage, pop-ups, papermaking, and paper sculpture. Weight: medium.

BRISTOL

Good-quality, fairly heavy paper, ideal for constructional purposes. Supplied in white and various colors. Suitable for collage, pop-ups, papermaking, and paper sculpture. Weight: heavy.

RECYCLED

Machine-made recycled papers are available in white and mainly pale colors. Suitable for weaving, collage, papercuts, pop-ups, papermaking, papier mâché, and paper sculpture. Weight: medium.

Commercial Uncoated: continued

SCORED

CURLED

CRUMPLED

TORN

PARCHMENT

Fine quality artwork paper available in unusual shades, such as peach and antique gold. Suitable for weaving, collage, papercuts, pop-ups, papermaking, papier mâché, and paper sculpture. Weight: medium.

KRAFT

Strong, low-cost wrapping paper, ribbed and unbleached. Suitable for weaving, collage, papercuts, papermaking, papier mâché, and paper sculpture. Weight: medium.

PASTEBOARD

Stiff and relatively thick unlined gray board. Suitable for collage, pop-ups, and papermaking. Weight: heavy.

NEWSPRINT

Coarse, weak paper used for newspapers and also sold for rough sketching. Usually white. Suitable for weaving, collage, papercuts, papermaking, papier mâché, and origami. Weight: standard.

Commercial Coated Papers

Handmade Papers

SCORED

CURLED

CRUMPLED

TORN

ART AND PRINTING PAPER
High-quality papers coated in gloss or dull finishes in a variety of colors. Suitable for weaving, collage, papercuts, pop-ups, and paper sculpture. Weight: heavy.

COVER PAPER
Firm, light, flexible coated cardboard in a wide range of colors. Suitable for weaving, collage, papercuts, pop-ups, and paper sculpture. Weight: heavy.

HANDMADE RAG LIGHT
Fine-quality, strong, durable white paper, available in cold-pressed, hot-pressed, and rough finishes. Suitable for weaving, collage, papercuts, papermaking, papier mâché, and paper sculpture. Weight: heavy.

HANDMADE RAG HEAVY
A heavier version of light rag paper with the same qualities and availability. Suitable for collage, pop-ups, papermaking, and paper sculpture. Weight: heavy.

Handmade Papers: continued

Specialty Papers

SCORED

CURLED

CRUMPLED

TORN

CHINESE HANDMADE
Superior paper suitable for weaving, collage, papercuts, papermaking, papier mâché, origami, and paper sculpture. Weight: variable.

HANDMADE WITH EMBEDDED OBJECTS
A variety of unusual effects and colors is possible with papers containing embedded items. Suitable for weaving, collage, papercuts, papier mâché, and paper sculpture. Weight: variable.

CREPE
Thin crinkled paper in white and various colors. Suitable for weaving, collage, papermaking, and papier mâché. Weight: standard.

TISSUE
Fine, easily crumpled paper, available in white and various colors. Suitable for weaving, collage, papermaking, papier mâché, and paper sculpture. Weight: standard.

SCORED

CURLED

CRUMPLED

TORN

TRACING
Highly transparent plain paper with a choice of thickness. Suitable for weaving, collage, origami, and paper sculpture. Weight: light and medium.

SUGAR PAPER
Inexpensive, plain paper in a variety of colors. Suitable for collage and weaving. Weight: standard.

CORRUGATED
Light but strong paper traditionally used as packing material for fragile items. Available in natural brown or various colors. Suitable for weaving, collage, pop-ups, papermaking, and paper sculpture. Weight: standard.

RICE PAPER
Thin paper made from rice grass, available in natural white. Suitable for weaving, collage, papermaking, and papier mâché. Weight: standard.

21

Tools and Equipment

MATERIALS

Most papercrafts require only basic tools, and you probably already own many of them. Tools for measuring and marking include pencils, rulers, a compass, and a triangle. You will also need scissors and knives — or a craft knife with interchangeable blades — for cutting. A cutting mat, although optional, is a good investment, because it saves wear on your knife blades and your work surface. Always use a metal ruler or straight-edge to guide your knife when cutting a straight line; a plastic ruler is not sturdy enough and could cause the blade to slip and cut you. At best, it will suffer damage itself and become unusable.

You will also want tools and materials to decorate your work, such as paints, pastels, brushes, and sprays. More specialized items for occasional use are shown on pages 26–27, but even some of those, or acceptable alternatives, may already be on hand around the house.

BASIC EQUIPMENT CHECK LIST

- ✓ Metal ruler
- ✓ Plastic ruler
- ✓ Triangle
- ✓ Craft knife
- ✓ Pencils – 2B and 6H
- ✓ Scissors, small and large
- ✓ Cutting mat
- ✓ Paint brushes
- ✓ Eraser
- ✓ Small wooden skewers

PAINTBRUSHES
1 in. (2.5 cm) brush for painting and glazing papier mâché and gluing collage components. Artists' brushes for finer detail.

CUTTING MAT
Self-sealing surface for smooth knife cutting and reduction of wear on blades.

KNIVES

A knife with interchangeable blades. You can also use a craft knife with a wedge-shaped blade for cutting straight strips and another with a long fine point for cutting intricate shapes.

TRIANGLE

For drawing straight lines and for use in conjunction with a ruler to draw parallel lines horizontally and vertically.

PENCILS

A 6H for transferring tracings and a 2B for drawing shapes on layout paper.

SMALL WOODEN SKEWERS

For applying small amounts of adhesive, especially useful in paper sculpture.

RULERS

A 12 in. (30 cm) plastic ruler for measuring and drawing and a 12 in. (30 cm) metal ruler for straight-edge cutting.

SCISSORS

Small scissors for detailed pieces and large scissors for cutting out basic shapes.

ERASER

White nylon eraser for removing pencil lines and any other unwanted marks.

Specialized tools

From time to time you will need to use a special piece of equipment: a hole punch to cut circles for eyes, a mold and deckle for papermaking, some foamcore to build relief effects. These pages show some of the specialized tools that paper artists find most useful, but you can also exploit your ingenuity to discover or improvise an item that works for a particular job. Our alternatives are listed in brackets.

ROLLER

For pressing large pieces of paper onto a background after gluing [rolling pin, dowel].

FOAMCORE

A sheet of foam, available in different thicknesses, used to elevate the paper layers and create relief effects [corrugated cardboard, polystyrene tiles].

LARGE SOFT BRUSH

For applying paste to paper [decorators' brush, paste brush].

NEEDLES

For piercing a pattern or making a small connecting hole, for example in mobiles [pins, thumbtacks].

PAPERMAKING EQUIPMENT

You must have the following pieces of equipment to make paper: mold and deckle (wooden frames for forming sheets of paper from pulped material); pressing boards (for pressing water out of freshly formed paper); pieces of felt (to layer between freshly made sheets when pressing).

Pressing boards [any board]

Felt [blanket or cloth]

Mold and deckle [embroidery frame]

You may be surprised to find that you already have much of the equipment needed, particularly for the papermaking section.

Bucket

Cat-litter tray

Liquidizer

Plastic palette knife

Hand-blender

Rubber gloves

Metal strainer

Plastic bowl

STAPLER
For fastening paper instantly. Useful for making quick models of a planned sculpture [paper clips].

WOODEN DOWEL
Used for shaping and curling paper [handle of wooden spoon].

WOODEN SCULPTING TOOLS
For scoring, curling, and general shaping [knitting needles, ballpoint pens].

BURNISHER
Ideal for flattening folds [empty ballpoint pen].

HOLE PUNCH/ LEATHER PUNCH
For punching small circles that would be difficult to cut out [paper punch].

MASKING TAPE
Useful for a variety of
purposes, but is more
temporary than glue.

Adhesives

A number of strong paper glues are
suitable for paper construction.
Polyvinyl acetate (PVA) or a quick-
bonding all-purpose adhesive is
recommended for pop-ups and
sculpture, and wallpaper paste or
white plastic glue are necessary for
papier mâché. Tape is useful for
temporary fixing.

**POLYVINYL ACETATE
(PVA)**
A good all-purpose
adhesive, particularly
for paper sculpture
and pop-ups.

Finishing

You will often want to add a
decorative finish to your art forms.
To create a good surface, coat
your work with gesso before
applying watercolor, acrylic,
or poster paints.

VARNISH
Make sure you use a
clear varnish to seal
paper, particularly for
decoupage.

PAINTS
The most useful paints
are watercolor, acrylic,
and poster paints.

GESSO
Available in tubs and
bottles. Used to seal
papier mâché before
painting.

Mold-Making

To build an original work in papier mâché, you will need materials for making a mold, and a releasing agent to prevent the paper from sticking to it.

WATERPROOF TAPE
Available in various colors and widths. Used for papermaking and casting.

SILICONE SEALANT
Used for casting paper and papier mâché.

VASELINE
Used for coating casts so that the mold releases easily.

MODELING CLAY
Used for making models for papier mâché.

FOUND OBJECTS

You can use found objects in a variety of ways for weaving, papier mâché, origami, collage, papermaking and paper sculpture. In addition to the items shown, you can experiment with twigs, leaves, bones, bark, seeds, wallpaper, junk mail, stones, leaflets, wrappers, washers, sand, fabric scraps – to mention just a few!

Old manuscript

Feathers

Wrapping papers

Brown paper

Dried flowers

String

Shells

Newspaper

2

Basic Techniques

Folding

Folding is one of the most elementary techniques of paper art, but there are numerous folds and ways of using them. We have probably all made an airplane by folding a piece of paper in half, matching the right side to the left, and creasing the center fold with our fingers. This is a basic fold, and it must be accurate. If your first fold is incorrect, subsequent folds will be affected, and the finished piece will look wrong. Many of the art forms in this book, such as Pop-Ups, Origami, Weaving, and Paper Sculpture, include folding. In this section we show you how to create simple accurate folds against a straightedge, how to pinch-fold by hand, and how to flatten a fold with tools such as a ruler, a roller, or a burnisher. Individual folds are shown in the Origami section (see pp. 74–89) and complex shapes in the scoring section (see pp. 38–39).

Before folding paper or cardboard, you should determine the direction of the grain – the alignment of the fibers in the paper. A fold will run smoothly with the grain but crookedly against the grain because the fibers are broken. You can check this by folding your sheet in both directions, but this wastes paper. Instead, bring together opposite edges of the sheet so that it curls; then do the same with the other two edges. You will form a tighter roll one way than the other, and this is the direction of the grain.

FLATTENING FOLDS

There are three ways to flatten a fold – especially important in making pop-ups and some origami forms. On diagrams, folds are indicated by dashed lines.

CREASING BY HAND
Run your thumb firmly along the fold. Repeat with your middle finger nail pushed by your thumb.

USING A RULER
Push the edge of a ruler firmly along the line of the fold. You can also use a burnisher (made of bone or plastic).

USING A ROLLER
Press the fold with an acrylic or rubber roller (available from most art supply stores).

A FOLDED PENGUIN

1 *Take a piece of thin paper 4 in. (10cm) square that is black on one side and white on the other. With the black side facing up, fold diagonally, corner to corner, to form a triangle. Flatten the fold with your fingers.*

2 *Reverse the fold so that the black faces up, and measure 2 in. (5cm) along the fold from the bottom corner. Take the corner and fold it upward so that the point touches your 2-in. (5-cm) mark. Crease the fold with your fingers.*

3 *Invert the diagonal fold so that you again have a white triangle with the bottom corner folded up inside the two halves. Bring the top open edge down about ½ in. (1.3cm) from the fold, and crease. Turn over and repeat.*

4 *Place a plastic triangle or ruler diagonally on the paper shape, about 1 in. (2.5cm) from the point. Fold the point upward, creasing it against the triangle edge. Remove the triangle, fold the point all the way down and crease.*

5 *Half open the body shape with one hand. Squeeze the point between the finger and thumb of your other hand to reverse the fold and form the head and beak of the penguin.*

6 *Check that both sides are perfectly even. Then flatten the fold you have just created, with your index finger.*

7 *Fold the penguin completely flat and press all folds again between your index fingers and thumbs.*

8 *Carefully open the center fold to reveal the penguin. Pull the wings slightly away from the body.*

9 *The finished penguin should show crisp folds, and stand up straight.*

Crumpling

I rregular creases can be used to form a 3-D structure, surface texture, and to enhance a background or a sculptural component. Bear in mind that crumpling greatly reduces the size of the paper. To build a 3-D structure, tightly crumple a flat sheet, then open it and model it into the desired shape. The creases allow you to shape the paper in virtually any direction, and by gathering, pleating, and pinching you can achieve some stunning abstract shapes. Another method is to begin with a regular geometric form, such as a cube, cylinder, or pyramid, and then completely crumple it. Reopen the form and carefully pull some of the wrinkles out from the crumpled surface to create a more organic,

naturalistic version of the original shape. Crumpled paper can also provide a softening contrast with regular textures. Lightweight papers are best for crumpling – usually the thinner the paper, the more successful the crumpled forms.

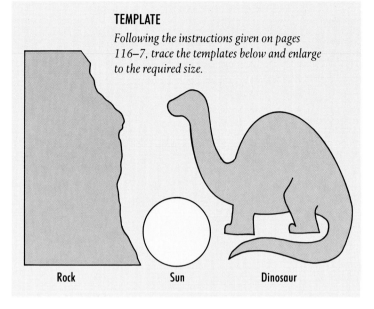

TEMPLATE
Following the instructions given on pages 116–7, trace the templates below and enlarge to the required size.

Rock   Sun   Dinosaur

CRUMPLED PAPER SWATCHES

Crumpling effects depend upon the paper used. Bond papers, such as most everyday stationery, allow sharp but light creases, whereas heavier cover papers give more pronounced effects. Cotton rag paper has no grain – its fibers are randomly distributed – so it can be modeled into soft creases. Layout paper, used by graphic artists to try out their ideas, is extremely light and malleable, but tracing paper is too brittle; the creases appear white and can split. Metallic or shiny papers reflect the light and can add interesting facets.

METALLIC PAPER

Light-reflecting, adding facets to crumpled work.

RAG PAPER

Gives soft creases, resists tearing, easy to paint.

LAYOUT PAPER

Light, translucent, and excellent for crumpling.

BOND PAPER

Fairly light; crumples in sharp surface wrinkles.

COVER PAPER

Varied colors; gives heavy, lasting creases.

TRACING PAPER

Thin, transparent, but too brittle to crumple.

A CRUMPLED DINOSAUR

1 On a piece of gray, medium- to lightweight paper, draw around the template using a black fineline marker. This will ensure that your outline is visible after you have crumpled the paper. Roll the paper into a crumpled ball.

2 Carefully unravel the ball of paper to avoid tearing it (you will notice that crumpling softens the paper), and with a small pair of scissors cut around the black outline.

3 Cut out a 4 in. (10cm) square piece of thin cardboard for the sky and a green rectangle with a torn top edge for the grass. Next draw a mountain shape on a piece of stone-colored paper and tear along the outline. Crumple all these pieces to add texture.

4 Apply a layer of silicone bathtub sealant to the reverse of the sun shape. This will be used on each component to act as an adhesive and as a support. Place the sun on the blue cardboard, pressing gently to fix it at the desired level.

5 Coat the back of each piece in turn with silicone sealant, working from the background to the foreground, adjusting the levels as necessary.

6 Finally, apply the sealant to the dinosaur and fix it in position. Set the finished piece aside for several hours to enable the sealant to dry.

Curling

BASIC TECHNIQUES

Different methods of curling paper reveal how light affects the surface of a work and gives it added dimension.

Identify and then follow the direction of the grain (see p. 36) where possible in order to manipulate the paper smoothly. Curl the paper by rolling it in your hands, or pull it over the straight edge of a table or over a scissors blade. Wind it around a wooden dowel or tightly around a small wooden skewer. Roll it tighter than you need it, because it always springs open slightly. When curling components – in paper sculpture, for example – cut them out before shaping them. You can tighten a curl by rewinding.

The method you use to curl paper will vary, depending on the length of the strip, the type of paper, and the effect required. In general, for small, tight curls use pressure or a small stick and for looser curls, relax the pressure or use a larger stick.

USING A SCISSORS BLADE
Curl cut-out components by pulling them against the scissors blade. Use your thumb to apply pressure. The harder you press, the tighter the end will be. Be careful, however, not to pull too hard, or the paper will tear.

TIGHTER CURLS
Use a small wooden skewer in the same way as the scissors, or roll the paper around it to achieve a tight curl. This works especially well with small pieces.

HAND PULLING
Keeping one hand on the paper while pulling it down over the edge of a table with the other is a good method for large strips.

TIPS FOR USING CURLED PAPER

✓ Pinch or crease basic curled shapes, such as coils, scrolls, and S-shapes, into hearts, triangles, and V-shapes.

✓ Use curled paper to decorate a greeting card with a seasonal motif, such as a candle.

✓ Cover the lid and side of a box with a pattern of curled shapes. Dense coils can make a strong surface that will not crush.

✓ Create a scene with curled forms, using strips of different widths to vary the relief. Craft stores carry ready-cut strips.

✓ Apply curled forms to an object by gluing the center of each shape and placing it in position. Tweezers or a toothpick will be a help.

✓ Try spraying a design with paint or varnish.

A CURLED SNAIL

1 Cut a strip of lightweight orange paper ⅛–¼ in. (3–6mm) wide and about 20 in. (51cm) long. You can join pieces by overlapping them by ⅛ in. (3mm) and attaching them with glue.

2 With a sharp craft knife, cut the tip off a wooden skewer and make a small slit in its place. Slide one end of the orange paper strip into the slit but do not let it protrude to the other side.

3 Coil the strip around the skewer in one revolution, and where the paper touches to complete the first layer apply glue. Continue to coil the strip evenly around the skewer until the end.

4 Take the coil off the skewer and form an eccentric coil. Tweezers are useful for holding the coil.

5 Holding the coil in place, apply a small dab of glue across all the layers to maintain the eccentric shape. Set aside until the glue dries.

6 Using a 10 in. (25.4cm) strip of green paper, repeat steps 4 and 5 on both sides to form a long thin oval. When set, pinch one end to form a point as shown.

9 Apply several dabs of glue to the underside of the eyes and position them on the head to complete your snail.

7 To make the eyes, coil green paper around the skewer 2½ times. Secure it with glue. Repeat, and attach eyes at the base of the stems. Hold the coils together with tweezers.

8 Holding the shell and body with tweezers, apply tiny dots of glue to the undersides. Position them on a piece of cardboard. Press them gently in place with your finger.

Tearing

**BASIC
TECHNIQUES**

Tearing offers a contrast to the hard edge of scissor- or knife-cuts and reveals the structure of the paper. You can tear paper as shown right or, if you want a straight edge, you can draw a line, place a ruler with its edge on the line and tear upward, away from the ruler and toward yourself. Tear with the grain if you want a straight line, or against the grain if you want an irregular look.

White paper coated with color will tear to reveal a white edge. Use a flash of white outline here and there to accentuate the color and give your work impact. You can control the amount of white by the way you tear the paper. Tearing away from yourself, colored side up, rips the paper on the reverse side and almost eliminates the white. Tearing toward you gives a distinct white edge.

Hold and tear the paper in the way that feels most comfortable. A right-hander, for example, will probably hold the paper in the left hand, with thumb on top and index finger underneath, tearing downward against the nail of the index finger.

Tearing shapes for sculpture and collage needs additional control. Score the shapes first with a stylus (see p. 22), being careful not to cut through the paper. You can then tear out the shape.

WITH THE GRAIN **AGAINST THE GRAIN**

To test for the grain, hold two adjacent edges of the sheet and bend it in half. Then take the other two edges and bend in half again. It is easier to bend with the grain than against it. This is true of all papers, although it is easier to see with a thicker paper.

WITH THE GRAIN **AGAINST THE GRAIN**

Tearing with the grain gives a smooth line that follows the fibers of the paper. Tearing against the grain creates a ragged effect because it breaks the fibers.

TEMPLATES
Following the instructions given on pages 116–7, trace the templates below and enlarge to the required size.

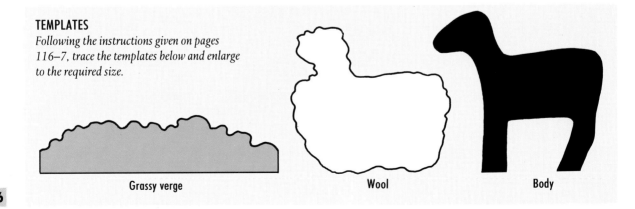

Grassy verge   Wool   Body

A TORN SHEEP

1 Trace the sheep's fleece template and transfer it onto a piece of medium-weight cream-colored paper. Then draw over the outline with a pointed stylus. This creates a groove of weakened fibers that will help you control your tearing. As you pull the paper apart, they will be the first to tear.

2 Cut around the fleece shape, leaving a margin of about 1 in. (25mm) all around. Hold the shape carefully in one hand moving your thumb along the draw line as you slowly tear around the image with the other. Pull the paper upward, against the thumb of your holding hand.

3 When you have torn all around the shape, neaten the edges by pinching away uneven bits of paper with your fingers or a pair of tweezers.

4 Repeat steps 1 to 3 on the black body and on the grass. The fine tips of grass will need extra care. When all the pieces are torn, use a toothpick to dab a few drops of glue on the black body, and adhere it to the back of the fleece.

5 Cut out a 4-in. (10-cm) square of pale blue paper and glue the grass strip to one edge. Dot some glue on the back of the completed sheep and attach it to the background, pressing firmly with your hand to flatten the image.

6 The torn ragged edges suggest the soft fleecy outline of wool far more effectively than a cleanly cut edge.

Scoring

Following the instructions given on pages 116–7, trace the templates below and enlarge to the required size.

Body   Shell

Scoring is used extensively in cardboard constructions, such as pop-ups and packaging, and is fundamental to paper sculpture. It enables you to create relief or build intricate pop-up mechanisms. Scoring also lends rigidity; the scored line acts like a spine to strengthen your creations.

There are two main types of scoring tool. The first is a stylus, or blunt-tipped instrument, which is pushed into the paper and pulled along a ruler or straightedge. The paper is then bent away from the indented line to create a well-defined, uniform fold. The second is a knife, used to cut a groove into the paper to weaken the area you want to fold. Practice this until you feel confident about the pressure required: if you press too hard, you will cut through the paper, and if you are too gentle, the fold will not be smooth. This method allows you to create curves that

appear to defy the limits of paper construction (see Paper Sculpture pp. 152–171). Our project shows you how to make a turtle, using both types of scoring tool. The shell is composed of multiple curved scores on a single piece of yellow-green medium-weight paper.

Experiment with different papers, cardboards, and shapes, and make a note of interesting discoveries so that you can incorporate them into future work. Keep some samples as a visual record, and you could build an exciting collection of geometric and organic shapes.

The purpose of scoring is to create a fault in the paper along which it will bend. There are several ways of achieving this.

INCISING

Run a craft knife lightly across the surface of the paper to carve a shallow incision. Bend the paper away from the cut.

PIERCING

Use the pointed tip of a craft knife to pierce a series of cuts in the paper. The thicker the paper, the closer the cuts should be.

BURNISHING

With a blunt stylus or a bone burnisher, score firmly along the paper and bend away from the score.

A SCORED TURTLE

1 Rule two intersecting lines from corner to corner of a 5-in. (12.7cm) square. Taking their intersection as your center, use a compass to draw a circle 4 in. (10cm) in diameter. Trace and transfer the fold lines from the shell template.

2 Cut out the circle. Score lightly with the tip of a craft knife on the inside and outside of all the curves except the two middle ones. These will lie at the head and tail of the turtle. Be careful not to cut through the paper.

3 Bend the paper away from the incised line to form a mountain fold (see p.53). Make sure that the entire curve folds back evenly by running your finger and thumb around it. Repeat this procedure on all the scored curves.

4 Score the remaining two curves with a blunt stylus. Turn the shell over. Define the indentations more clearly by bending the paper away from them. You now have one mountain fold and two valley folds in each side of the shell.

5 To make the two mountain folds as crisp as the valley folds, score the indented lines with a craft knife just enough to make a small incision in the paper. Turn over and score the two remaining curves top and bottom.

6 Bend paper away from the top and bottom scored curves, holding the sides between your fingers and thumbs as shown. Push the sides toward each other slightly to form the finished shell.

7 Trace the body template, transfer it to a piece of brown medium-weight paper and cut it out. Score all the lines from the back with a blunt stylus. The tail will form a mountain fold and the flippers will show indentations.

8 Put two dabs of glue on the underside of the shell in the middle of the mountain folds. Turn the shell over and place it on top of the body. Press the glue points with the blunt stylus until they adhere firmly.

9 The finished turtle gains its dimension from the variety of incised and indented lines.

Embossing

TEMPLATES
Following the instructions given on pages 116–7, trace the template and enlarge to the required size.

BASIC TECHNIQUES

Embossing is the technique of adding relief to paper by burnishing with a stylus or a round-tipped tool over a raised shape, such as a cardboard cut-out. You can see many examples of embossing on greetings cards, expensive letterheads, invitations, and book covers.

In the printing industry, there are several different embossing terms: a blind emboss, a printed emboss, and a multi-level emboss. A blind emboss is an embossed image on a plain piece of paper without the use of a printed image. For a printed emboss, the image is first printed on the paper and then embossed with a simple raised shape on one level. This treatment gives the printed image an added dimension. The multi-level emboss is just that – an embossed image with varying levels. This is the most expensive form of embossing since it requires handmade metal dies.

Using variations of these methods, you can create delightful embossed images of your own with a minimum of equipment. By following the step-by-step demonstration of the dolphin you will see how easy and effective embossing is. Try experimenting with thicker and thinner cardboard shapes and gluing together different levels of cardboard to create your own multi-level emboss. The important thing to remember is to keep most of your corners slightly rounded as it is difficult to get the burnishing tool into sharp corners. Watercolor papers made of 100 per cent cotton rag are the best to use, as they will withstand more handling before they tear.

WET AND DRY EMBOSSING

You can obtain satisfactory results with dry embossing, and you will not have to wait for it to dry. However, you will find that you can push the paper to greater limits when you dampen it first.

DRY PAPER

As the stylus marks clearly show, you will need to press harder with dry paper. But take care not to tear the paper.

DAMP PAPER

This example demonstrates the greater detail possible when you dampen the paper – the lines of the fin are sharper.

AN EMBOSSED DOLPHIN

1 *Transfer the tracing of the template onto a piece of medium-weight cardboard 6 in. (15cm) square. Use a sharp blade to cut out the background outline, including the internal form of the dolphin and the water droplets.*

2 *Glue the cut-out background to another 6 in. (15cm) square of cardboard. This will act as a base to hold all the cutouts together. Paste the two halves of the dolphin into place on the base.*

3 *Measure and draw a 4-in. (10-cm) square around your assembled embossing jig to enable you to position your paper accurately on top of it.*

4 *Immerse a 4-in. (10-cm) square of blue medium-weight paper in a tray of water.*

5 *Blot excess moisture with paper towel, leaving the sheet damp and flexible. Store additional squares between moist pieces of paper towel if you want to make several impressions of the same emboss.*

6 *Align the damp sheet carefully on the pencilled square. Because it is wet you can't tape it in position, so hold it firmly while embossing.*

7 *Using a round ball burnishing tool, gently rub the paper into the cut-out shape. Work cautiously to sense the correct degree or pressure: too much and the paper will tear; too little and the embossed line will be ill-defined.*

8 *When you can see the image clearly in negative (from the back), carefully peel away the paper from the top, keeping your other hand on the opposite bottom corner.*

9 *The finished boss should look like this, with distinct, well-formed, swelling lines. The cardboard jig can be reused several times.*

Cutting

Good cutting can make the difference between a well-finished piece of work and a jagged, untidy one – as anyone who has cut out a circle freehand will know. The two tools for cutting paper are scissors and craft knives. Both have their merits for particular tasks, but generally you should choose whichever you feel more comfortable using.

There are numerous hobby or craft knives, but the best choice is the type with a choice of handles to which you can fit a range of interchangeable blades, such as the X-Acto knife. Blades should include the long, sharp, finely-pointed frisket blade, designed for clean cutting without pressure, and a mat blade for sturdier work. A round handle is preferable to a flat-sided one, as rolling in your fingers as you cut can make it easier to achieve flowing curves. You will also need three pairs of scissors: an 8 in. (20cm) pair, a 4 in. (10cm) pair, and some small needlework scissors for fine detail. It is easier to make accurate

TEMPLATE
Following the instructions given on pages 116–7, trace the template and enlarge to the required size.

scissor cuts by keeping the scissors fixed in one hand and feeding the work through them with the other hand. Scissors will not cut through materials heavier than medium-weight paper and lightweight cardboard, however; for these you must use a frisket knife or a craft knife fitted with the appropriate blade.

Hold the knife as if it were a pen. This gives you greater control. Practice rolling the handle as you cut, so that you are not limited by the movement of your wrists when cutting a tight curve. In cutting, practice makes perfect.

SCISSORS

Keep the scissors still and turn the paper into the path of the blades. This method produces more accurate cuts than keeping the paper still and moving the scissors.

KNIFE

A sharp blade always gives a crisp edge. With a little practice you will find it as comfortable as using a pencil, enabling you to make flowing curves. Use a cutting mat to save wear on your blade and damage to furniture.

42

A CUTOUT ZEBRA

1 *Draw the zebra directly onto white paper 4 in. (10cm) square, or transfer the template so that it appears in reverse (facing right). That way there will be no pencil marks to erase when you turn your cutout over.*

2 *Begin cutting out the traced shapes, keeping all the lines crisp and flowing. Cut completely into corners, so that the shapes drop out neatly.*

3 *To cut a thin pointed shape, work downward from both sides to meet at the point. This avoids pulling at the fine detail, which could cause creasing.*

4 *You can then lift the shape out with the tip of your knife blade.*

5 *Continue cutting until you have completed the zebra head.*

6 *Take a 4-in. (10-cm) square of black paper to serve as your background. Apply dots of glue to the underside of the cutout with a toothpick.*

7 *Place the cutout sheet over the black paper, lining up the left-hand side and the top. When it is accurately positioned, press it with your hand or flatten it with a roller. Allow the glue to dry.*

8 *At the end of step 5, you were left with a small piece that was not connected to the rest of the head. Use it to form the bottom right corner. Glue it into position and press it down with your finger.*

9 *The finished head should be a crisp, clear image, with no glue visible on the black paper.*

Piercing

BASIC TECHNIQUES

Piercing is a means of creating surface texture. A variety of tools can be used, including pins, knives, punches, tracing wheels, knitting needles, and a stylus. The only limit to your options is your imagination.

You can create an entire design by piercing or use it as a partial effect. Geometric designs are easy to make with the aid of squared paper. Draw a pattern of dots at the intersections of the squares on a sheet of graph paper. Place the sheet over a piece of colored paper, attach the two to a foamcore (polystyrene) board, and push pins through your design. Foamcore is the best support for all piercing methods, because sharp points sink easily into it, ensuring a clean cut, without damaging your work surface. Incised patterns can be raised

TEMPLATES
Following the instructions given on pages 116–7, trace the templates and enlarge to the required size.

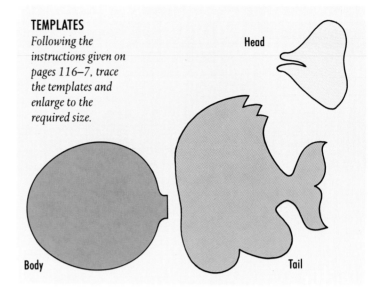

Head

Body

Tail

from the paper to give added texture to designs and backgrounds, or greater realism to features such as feathers and scales. Make your own reference file of textures by using a variety of piercing tools on a white sheet of watercolor paper. Label each mark to identify the tool that made it. Experiment with different effects.

PIERCING METHODS

Anything that you can push through paper can be used to add texture – from nails and knitting needles for rough marks to pins and knives for fine holes and slits.

You will find it easier to work with a needle if you push a small cork over the blunt end. Place paper on a piece of foamcore (polystyrene) board.

SMALL HOLES
Piercing with needles of different thicknesses produces the effect of a dot-screen picture as seen in newspapers. The closer the dots, the blacker the area, and vice versa.

CRAFT KNIFE PIERCING
A pointed craft knife blade gives a thin vertical wedge shape. This can be used in a series of alternating rows to create unusual patterns.

LARGER HOLES
Larger holes can be achieved with numerous tools, such as a blunt stylus, an awl, dried-up ballpoint pens, nails, knitting needles, or sharpened wooden dowels.

PUNCHING
Leather punches create interesting borders, but you are limited to the edge of the paper by the maximum opening of the punch.

A PIERCED FISH

1 *Transfer the traced image of the round body part onto a piece of red paper and make the V-shaped cuts with a sharp craft knife. Be careful not to overcut near the edge of the paper or you will weaken the shape.*

2 *Hold the edges between fingers and thumbs and curl the paper back. The V-shapes pop out to form raised scales.*

3 *From the back, pierce alternate scales with a needle, making a triangle of six holes (three, two, and one). Apply knife slits to the remaining scales, forming a triangle of three slits on each.*

4 *Curl back the edges again to see the effect of this patterning.*

5 *Transfer the tracing of the fins and tail assembly onto orange paper. Pierce needle holes along the lines of the tail, and a hole at the end of each fin line. Cut from these holes to the end of each pierced line with a craft knife.*

6 *Using a toothpick, apply a line of glue along the edges of the orange part. Place the red section on top, curving slightly so that scales protrude. Cut out the head, pierce its detail with a needle, and glue it into position.*

7 *On a piece of 4 in. (10cm) square pale blue paper, pierce bubble shapes of varying size with a needle. Create a shadow on one side of each bubble by piercing three rows of holes.*

8 *Put two dabs of glue on the reverse of the fish, one at the front of the head and one at the base of the tail. Glue the fish to the blue square, leaving a slight curl in the middle so that it retains shape. Lift some scales with a knife.*

9 *The completed fish gains its effect from a variety of pierced patterns that are accentuated by light and shade.*

Coloring

The advantage of coloring paper yourself is that you can achieve exactly the shade or effect that you want. You can do this by brush painting, sponging, spattering, color washing, and marbling.

Sponging works best with watercolor paper, a natural sponge and the vinyl paints used in producing animated films. If you cannot find these, use artist's acrylics.

Spattering mottles the paper surface, giving visual weight to the work. Marbling can create rich and original patterns. You can use aerosol paints, oil paint diluted with turpentine, or drawing inks (see opposite).

Often you need a specific color to complete a project. If you can't find the right ready-made shade, the only answer is to color the paper yourself. You can do this in several ways: brush painting, sponging, spattering, color washing, and marbling (see opposite).

TEMPLATES
Following the instructions given on pages 116–7, trace the templates and enlarge to the required size.

Top wings

Lower wings

Body

BRUSH PAINTING
When using a special color for a component – in a paper sculpture, for example – cut the piece from white paper before painting with acrylic or watercolor. That way you can also color the edges.

SPONGING
Mix paint to a light creamy consistency and dip a sponge into it. Dab the excess onto a piece of newspaper until you see the texture and depth of color that you want. Apply the sponge to your paper in random dabs.

SPATTERING
Spattering gives a project texture, and is similar to a coarse airbrush effect. Load a toothbrush with color and point it downward toward the paper. Draw a piece of stiff cardboard toward you over the bristles, so that they flick paint onto the paper.

COLOR WASHES
For successful color washes, wet the paper first and stretch it on a wooden board, holding it down with gummed paper tape. Allow the paper to dry thoroughly before washing color over it with a wide watercolor brush.

A MARBLED BUTTERFLY

1 *Half-fill a tray with water. Scatter the surface with a few random drops of waterproof blue ink. As they begin to spread, add some drops of red.*

2 *With a needle, gently swirl one color into the other. The movements of your needle are reflected in the pattern of the inks. Try clockwise and counter-clockwise actions until you are happy with the result.*

3 *Hold a piece of watercolor paper by diagonally opposite corners. Keeping hold of the corners, lower a free corner onto the water surface, followed in one smooth movement by the rest of the paper.*

4 *As soon as the paper touches the surface, begin lifting it off in reverse order, picking up the opposite corner first and peeling away. Turn the sheet over. If necessary, repeat the process.*

5 *Trace the butterfly template onto a piece of scrap paper and cut it out to make a template of your own. This can be moved around over the marbled pattern until you find an area you like for the butterfly wings.*

6 *Draw the two separate wing outlines on the marbled paper and cut them out with a craft knife. Save the spare paper for another project.*

7 *Cut the butterfly body out of gray paper and spatter it with blue ink. Score a line down the center and fold it in half to form a V. Then score a line down the center of each wing and fold forward in a slight V shape.*

8 *Glue the two sets of wings into position along the score line. Use a toothpick to put a dot of glue on each side of the body's underside and attach it to the top of the wing assembly.*

9 *The finished butterfly. Try the same project with a different pair of coloring techniques.*

Menagerie Sampler

BASIC TECHNIQUES

At this point in the book you should possess nine splendid animal motifs covering all the basic techniques. It would be a pity to leave them on a shelf collecting dust or to hide them away in a drawer, so why not display them in a shadow box frame as a reminder of the techniques? This display frame design can be adapted for all the projects in the book. If you are a confident woodworker, you can construct a simple wooden frame with nine divisions. Alternatively, you could ask a picture framing store to make one for you.

We show you, here, how to make a basic foamcore box. Simply follow the step-by-step instructions and add a finish of your choice. When gluing the animals to the backing board, first glue small blocks of foamcore to the back of each. When your menagerie is complete, hang the framed work in a place of honor. Remember not to expose it to direct sunlight as the paper colors will fade.

DISPLAYING YOUR MENAGERIE

When arranging your creatures in the frame, you need to consider color, lighting, shapes, and textures. Some will require a background, others will need to be raised with ½ in. (10mm) foamcore blocking.

A CUTOUT ZEBRA

Cutting, pages 42–3
A layer of foamcore flat against the back of the frame raises the zebra slightly.

A SCORED TURTLE

Scoring, pages 38–9
An earthy textured backing paper complements the colors of the snail. With a dab of glue stick attach a small oblong piece of foamcore to raise the turtle above the background. This will give more interesting shadow and depth.

A TORN SHEEP

Tearing, pages 36–7
The sheep is raised slightly by inserting a backing of thin foamcore.

MAKING THE BOX

1 *Cut four strips of foamcore 2 x 12½ in. (7.6 x 31.7cm). Make two ¼ x 1¼ in. (0.6 x 3.2cm) slits in each piece 4 in. (10cm) from each end.*

2 *Slot the four pieces together to make nine square divisions. Add glue to the bottom edge of each and press down on a 13 x 13 in. (33 x 33cm) foamcore base.*

3 *Cut two pieces of 3 x 26 in. (7.6 x 66cm) foamcore. Score lightly with a craftknife half way along each strip. Bend them in half. Glue the two right-angled pieces to the base to form walls.*

A CRUMPLED DINOSAUR
Crumpling, pages 32–3
The dinosaur has dimension and texture and can just be displayed flat against the frame base.

AN EMBOSSED DOLPHIN
Embossing, pages 40–1
Two layers of foamcore raise the dolphin above the shadow cast by the frame so that the light catches the embossing.

A MARBLED BUTTERFLY
Coloring, pages 46–7
A white textured background paper sets off the colors. Raise the butterfly with a narrow strip of foamcore glued to the base so that the head is higher than the body.

A CURLED SNAIL
Curling, pages 34–5
Like the dinosaur, the snail needs no blocking and is displayed flat against the frame base.

A FOLDED PENQUIN
Folding, pages 30–1
A charcoal gray background paper complements the color of the dinosaur. As the most three-dimensional of the creatures, the penquin dictates the depth of the box. It fits snugly into the compartment.

A PIERCED FISH
Piercing, pages 44–5
Raise the fish with a layer of foamcore. Then carefully raise the pierced areas with a blade so that the light catches them.

3

Art Forms

Pop-ups

Most of us remember child-hood books whose stories were brought to life with wonderful pop-up pictures. Today, many of us receive greeting cards whose message pops up when the card opens. Some are so ingenious that you want to go on playing with them and discover how they are constructed.

There are ten basic mechanisms for pop-ups, and these act as a starting point for all the variations found in books and cards. Using these mechanisms you can create images that spring up, slide, rotate, and move in a variety of ways. Here we show you how to make single slit, double-slit in two variations, multi-slit, pull-up planes, moving arm, v-fold, and dissolving scenes. The remaining three mechanisms (magic box, rotating disk, and pivoting motion) are complicated and are best tried only after you are thoroughly familiar with the ones in this book.

It is especially important when constructing pop-ups to make sure that your measurements,

scores, cuts, and folds are accurate, or the mechanism will not work. Use a triangle, ruler, and protractor to keep scoring straight and square. It helps to make one or two roughs before attempting your finished design.

Whenever you see a pop-up mechanism that you find interesting and may want to use at a later date, make some notes or a rough copy of it and file it for reference.

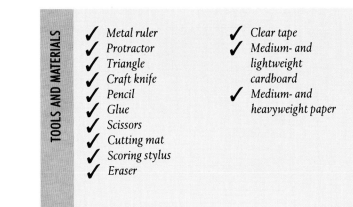

TOOLS AND MATERIALS

✓ Metal ruler
✓ Protractor
✓ Triangle
✓ Craft knife
✓ Pencil
✓ Glue
✓ Scissors
✓ Cutting mat
✓ Scoring stylus
✓ Eraser

✓ Clear tape
✓ Medium- and lightweight cardboard
✓ Medium- and heavyweight paper

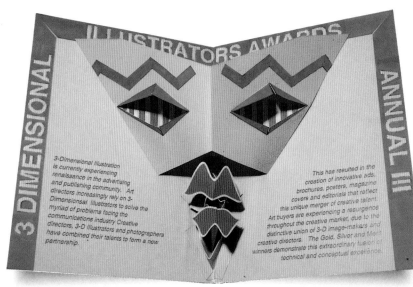

COMBINING TECHNIQUES

This pop-up is a mix of several mechanisms. The ingenious design of the lips resembles that of a rose and produces a striking image overall (Année Galtier).

A V-FOLD POP-UP

The artist used extensive decoration around the main mechanism to great effect. This composition explodes with life and color (Theresa Pindroh).

SIMPLE COMPLEXITY

The success of this card is based on meticulous measurement. Cut from a simple rectangle and creased with a bone folder, the mechanism moves forward and backward (Paul Jackson).

POP-UP TECHNIQUES

CUT LINES

Cuts are indicated by a continuous line. Use a knife for pop-ups, making sure that you start at the beginning of the line and finish at the end.

VALLEY FOLDS

A valley fold is folded upward. These folds are shown by a broken line.

MOUNTAIN FOLDS

A mountain fold folds back to form a peak. These folds are indicated by a line of dashes and dots.

Single Slit

The single-slit mechanism is composed of a series of valley and mountain folds. It works across the center fold of the card, turning part of it from a valley fold into a mountain fold. This is the basis for several pop-up effects. The slit can be any shape and begin anywhere on the central fold provided the end of it is connected to the central fold by a scored fold.

1 Fold a piece of cardboard in half and make a horizontal cut from the fold halfway across the sheet, making sure that you cut through both layers of cardboard.

2 Score a diagonal line from the fold to the end of the cut line. Do the same above the cut line.

3 Fold both scored lines forward to form a V. Flatten the folds with your thumbs, then fold them down again so that the cut lines meet.

4 Turn the card over and repeat step 3, folding both scored lines firmly back the other way, and then flat again.

5 Opening up the card, you will have one cut line and four scored lines forming a diamond pattern across the center fold.

6 Holding the bottom of the card, pull the top part of the diamond forward from the cut line to fold inward. Repeat with the bottom half of the diamond. Then close the card.

7 Flatten both inverted folds with your index finger to establish their direction.

8 Opening and closing the card will cause the diamond shape to work in reverse. It will open as you close the card, and close when you open it. This is also the basis for the moving arm mechanism.

Double Slit – Symmetrical

This technique is similar to the one used for single slit (left) but allows for greater creative scope. Basically it always has two slits in the central fold. These can be any shape and are connected by a fold. This fold does not have to be parallel to the central crease.

1 *Fold a rectangular piece of cardboard in half. With the fold to the left, make two horizontal slits through both thicknesses of the cardboard from the fold to half-way across the card. Fold the center flap to the left as shown.*

2 *Fold the flap back again and open the card. Pull the central flap forward from the fold. Close the card, pressing the front with your hand. When you open and close the card the flap will open and close in the opposite direction.*

Double Slit – Asymmetrical

The pop-ups shown so far spring symmetrically from a central fold. This variation of the double slit pops up to one side, or asymmetrically. Instead of working through both folded halves of the card at the same time, we must now work on the unfolded card and measure the construction lines precisely to achieve a smooth mechanism.

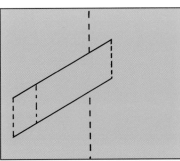

1 *On some cardboard 8½ x 11 in. (21.5–28cm) lightly draw the lines as shown. Make sure that measurements are accurate. You will end up with four valley folds, one mountain fold, and two parallel cut lines.*

2 *Check that all the lines on the mechanism are parallel. Then, with a craft knife and metal ruler, cut along the full length of both cut lines.*

3 *Using your scoring stylus, score the two valley folds along the central strip, and the one mountain fold. Then score either side of the slit section and the two central valley folds.*

4 *Hold the card up and close it slightly as you pull the mountain fold forward between the cut-out section.*

5 *Pinch the valley folds at each end of the slit section to flatten them. Close the card, making sure that the mountain fold comes forward as you do so. Then flatten all folds on the closec card.*

55

Multi-slit – Asymmetrical

This multi-slit is simply a pair of double-slit pop-ups of diminishing size. It is possible to make a continuing series by adding more pairs of slits, which in turn will create more mountain and valley folds. But the more folds you create, the harder the card will be to open and close.

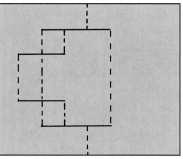

1 *Carefully measure and draw the above configuration on any piece of cardboard. Number the slits 1 to 4 to save confusion. You will end up with a stepped pop-up of three mountain folds and six valley folds.*

2 *Cut the four slits, using a craft knife and a metal ruler: from 1–1, 2–2, 3–3, 4–4. Keep all cuts straight and parallel. Score all the fold lines with a stylus along a ruler. Be careful not to score through the center fold.*

3 *Hold the card in both hands, and close it slightly while pushing the valley fold 1–2 from behind to establish the longest fold.*

4 *Holding the end at right angles, pull the three mountain folds forward and up, so that the pop-up step is at 90° to the card.*

5 *Close the card and flatten all folds from the back with your thumb to establish the finished pop-up.*

6 *Open the card to test the mechanism. When the card is opened at 90°, all folds should be correspondingly at 90° and form three neat steps.*

MULTI-SLIP POP-UP

The multi-slit mechanism is useful because it makes a good foundation for more complex pop-up shapes. When attaching a shaped piece to the mechanism, open the card so that the two halves are at right angles, then you will clearly see where to seat the base of the piece you are sticking on; otherwise you will end up with a gap at the bottom.

Pull-up Planes

This device is often used in pop-up books to reveal a hidden image. It works on the lever principle. Pulling the paper tab at the bottom causes a flap of paper to lift up as a fold pulls against the top slot.

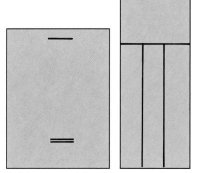

1 *Measure and draw on a piece of cardboard the artwork shown above.*

2 *Use a craft knife and metal ruler to cut out the pop-up flap and pull tab.*

3 *Run a metal stylus along the fold line a couple of times to establish a definite score.*

4 *Holding the pop-up flap in one hand, bend the tab along the scored line and flatten the fold.*

5 *Take the second piece of cardboard, which will form the base. Cut out the slot at the top. Then cut the slit for the tab to return through. Finally make the cut at the bottom.*

6 *Holding the base in one hand, pass the tab through the top slot from the front until it reaches the fold.*

7 *Return the tab through the bottom slit so that it forms a pull handle at the front.*

8 *Pull the tab downward as you hold the card and the flap will raise like a trapdoor.*

Moving Arm Pop-Up

The moving arm mechanism is constructed by attaching a stick-on arm to the standard "V" fold. When you open the card the arm moves up to point at the greeting or graphic. By using imagination, you can turn the arm into other graphic shapes.

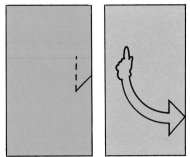

1 Trace the template of the arm, transfer it to a piece of orange cardboard and cut it out. Take a piece of blue cardboard measuring 8 x 6 in. (203 x 152mm), and fold in half to create a card 6 x 4 in. (152 x 101mm).

2 Place the arrowhead on the folded edge of the card, making sure that the hand does not exceed the bottom edge of the card. Trace the arrowhead onto card.

3 Using a sharp blade, cut one side of the arrowhead through the two thicknesses of cardboard. Score its counterpart gently with a craft knife.

4 Fold back the cut flap along the scoreline. Then turn the cardboard over and fold the flap back the other way to establish a clear fold in both thicknesses.

5 Open the card. Pull the top of the cut flap forward with your finger and close the card to establish the mechanism.

6 Align the arrow end of the arm with the left side of the cut flap to check that it fits and that the hand will not stick out from the top of the closed card.

7 Glue the underside of the arrowhead onto the flap. Hold the arm in place for a few seconds until the glue is dry, then pull the arm forward and close the card.

8 When you open the card the arm should raise and point to the top.

V-fold

This mechanism is widely used in pop-up books and greeting cards. It consists of a folded shape glued to the card from left to right across the fold. Tabs are used to attach it. When closed, the "V" shape folds into the central fold of the card and when opened it stands perpendicular to the surface of the card.

1 Trace the cloud template onto a piece of blue paper and cut out the profile.

2 Make the small incision at the center of the bottom edge with a knife.

3 Using a stylus and straight-edge or ruler, score all the fold lines. Fold the cloud in half along the center line.

4 Fold the bottom glue tab up and crease it with your finger. Then fold the tab up on the reverse side.

5 Take a piece of yellow card and fold it down the middle. Glue one tab of cloud.

6 Position the cloud diagonally on the card, with glued flap downward, making sure that the left edge touches the center fold. Press it firmly for a few seconds until dry. Glue the facing flap into place.

7 Close the card and apply pressure until the glue sets.

8 When you open the card, the cloud will stand up in a V shape; hence the name V-fold.

Skyline Pop-up

Constructing a pop-up scene •

Creating depth using three floating layers •

Creating background and foreground •

Everyone is fascinated by pop-ups, whether it be a simple greeting card or a magical children's pop-up book. This project employs a mechanism that has been used extensively in both of these applications and is fundamental to the creation of most pop-ups.

The floating layers mechanism permits paper layers to float or project parallel to the base plane. This allows you to create an effective sense of depth using only three layers of paper as demonstrated here. The base plane can be perceived in two ways. If it is vertical, as in this project, the layers float in front of the base. If perceived as horizontal, then the layers float above it (for example, a butterfly on a flower).

The mechanism needs three vertical supports of the same height, attached one at each end, and one at the center fold. It helps to make roughs using medium-weight paper that can be folded easily by hand. This way, you can experiment with the mechanism and perfect your folds and supports before using your good heavy-weight paper to construct the final pop-up.

When you've completed this project, you may wish to explore the technique further and invent your own variations. It helps to look through pop-up books to identify the floating layers mechanism and see to what ingenious limits you can push it.

A floating-layer pop-up makes a spectacular greeting card. This design would suit a romantic occasion.

TEMPLATES

Trace from these templates, enlarged to the size you require, to assemble your pieces. The dotted lines indicate folding lines.

Front skyline

Yellow disk

Supports

Back skyline

Costumes

Dancers

Blue foreground

Cloud

CONSTRUCTION DIAGRAM

Here you can see how the separate layers, which appear to float independently of one another, are actually anchored to each other and to the base by supports.

Pop-up image

Floating layers

Base

Support flaps

Supports

Support flaps

1 *Begin by tracing all of the templates. Transfer the tracing onto lightweight cardboard in the colors of your choice. Carefully cut out all the shapes using a sharp knife and a metal straight edge.*

2 *With a stylus, score the background skyline along the fold marks. You may need to run the stylus along the pencil line a couple of times to establish a definite scored line. Fold one edge inward as shown.*

3 *Repeat this procedure on the other edge to complete the first of the three layers. These tabs will elevate the skyline layer from the cardboard background.*

4 *Using a ruler, find the mid-point of the skyline, and draw a vertical line down it with a pencil. This will be the point at which this layer folds.*

5 *Hold a metal straight edge along the pencil line and score the line with a stylus to establish the folding point.*

6 *Fold the skyline neatly in half along the scored center line. Run your finger and thumb along the fold a couple of times to establish a good, crisp fold.*

7 Since this first layer is wide you will need to attach a support behind the center line to prevent the layer from sagging in the middle. Cut out and score the center support. This will match the depth of the two end supports.

8 Neatly fold the support between your fingers and thumbs along the scored lines to create a three-sided support.

9 Glue one edge of the support and paste it to the right side of the skyline center fold as shown. Run your finger along the back of the glued edge to make certain it adheres properly.

10 Accurately position the skyline on the inside, left side of the card, carefully aligning the bottom edges and butting the center support right up to the center fold of the card. Accuracy at this stage is critical to the subsequent layers and the operation of the card.

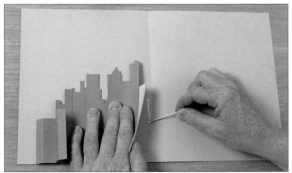

11 Lift the support while holding the skyline in place. Carefully glue the card beneath, and press down until glue has set and the position of the central support is established.

12 Fold the left tab down and apply glue to it. Close the card to adhere the tab firmly in position. Do the same with the right tab.

13 Repeat steps 2–12 on the front skyline layer, gluing it to the background skyline layer. It is important to be accurate when positioning one layer on the other.

14 Take the cut-out cloud. Score the straight side along the fold lines with a metal straight edge and stylus. Crease between fingers and thumbs.

15 Make the interlocking incision with a knife. This will hold the cloud in place without using glue. As long as one edge is glued to the background, the skyline layer will pull the cloud into position when the card is opened.

16 Using small scissors, cut a 1 in. (25mm) slit halfway up the background skyline support from the card surface. This will accommodate the slit you made in the cloud.

17 Apply glue to the folded support on the side of the cloud. You will need to work quite fast. The cloud must be positioned before the glue sets.

18 Carefully slide the cloud into position, interlocking the two slits on the right while holding the support at right angles to the cloud. Close the card and firm down.

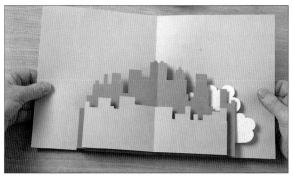

19 *Check the mechanism by opening the card. The layers should rise parallel to the base and not lean to one side. The depth of the scene is governed by the height of the supports.*

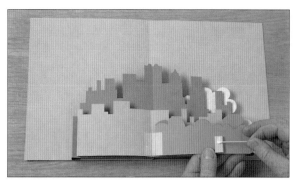

20 *Glue one half of the central support to the back of the blue foreground, and the other half to the skyline center fold. Then attach one end support flap and close the card to adhere it firmly. Repeat with the third support.*

21 *When you open the card you should have four layers, including the white cloud, that rise smoothly from the background and create a wonderful feeling of depth.*

22 *Assemble the cutouts for the dancers and paste them to the pink base. Details can be positioned with the point of a knife. If you are using polyvinyl acetate glue you will need to work quickly before it dries.*

23 *Roll the pieces with a good hard roller so that they stick flat to the base. If you have any edges that are not stuck, add some glue with the point of a toothpick and re-roll.*

24 *Glue the dancers to the yellow disk and attach the unit to the blue foreground. Make sure that the woman's elbow remains on the left of the center fold so that the card closes.*

Season Change

Making an accurate sliding mechanism •

Dissolving one scene into another •

Concealing the mechanism •

ART
FORMS

Sliding mechanisms make it possible for you to dissolve one scene and create another. This type of mechanism offers great design potential. The intricate sliding construction calls for care and accuracy. You will need to use your protractor to create the angles required for smooth operation. The mechanism consists of two pieces: a base with five parallel angled cuts, and a moving section with parallel angled cuts that interweave with the base cuts. Sliding the moving section back and forth reveals either its picture or the one on the base.

Draw and color your designs before you cut the parallel strips. If you use photographs mounted on cardboard, glue them firmly, so that they will not catch when you slide the mechanism. The pictures here show a change in season, but could be any two images that suit your fancy.

This project may look complicated at first but provided your measurements are accurate, you should have no difficulty creating a mechanism that transforms one image beautifully into another.

TEMPLATES

Minor variations in the size of the sun and clouds are unimportant, but the two pieces that operate the sliding mechanism must be exactly as shown for the movement to work.

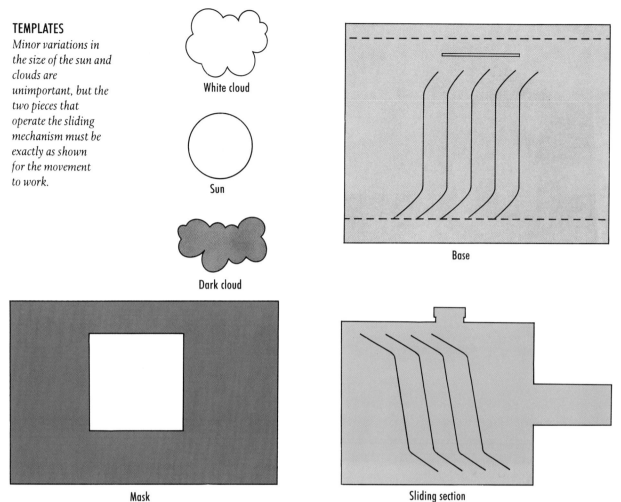

White cloud

Sun

Dark cloud

Base

Mask

Sliding section

CONSTRUCTION

The mechanism underlying the graphics comprises two pieces of cardboard that slide through each other by means of interlocking slits. These are framed by a mask that provides additional decoration. Add glue only at the corners.

Mask

Sliding blue section

Base

1 Cut the side and top slits in the pale gray card. Then cut the four central tabs, leaving them attached at the bottom.

2 Turn the card over. Score the top and bottom folding lines lightly with a craft knife and fold back. Held up, the card should look like this.

3 Cut the three central tabs in the blue sliding piece but leave them attached at top and bottom. Fold the lower tab of the handle up, and the upper part down, to form a triple thickness, and glue into place.

4 Cut out the cloud and sun, paste them into position on the blue card, and roll them flat.

5 Turn the blue card over and cut the slits again to include the sun and cloud. Check from the right side that you have cut all the way through.

6 Glue the dark cloud onto the gray card. Punch out some white paper snowflakes with a leather or paper punch, and add these to the gray card.

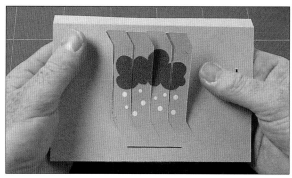

7 *Repeat step 5, cutting the slits through from the back.*

8 *Holding the gray card reverse side up, insert the top tab of the blue card into the slot as shown.*

9 *Insert the four gray central tabs into the slots of the blue card, one by one, and then place it flat on the table with the reverse side up.*

10 *With the blue and gray cards in position as shown, put a dot of glue on the end of each gray central tab and fold the gray edge up to attach. Glue and fold the top edge down so that it does not touch the blue card.*

11 *Cut a mask to hide the mechanism, and glue it on top of the gray card at the four corners.*

12 *Cutting and gluing everything precisely should ensure that the mechanism operates smoothly. If your paper graphics catch when sliding, try painting them on instead.*

Lion in a Cage

ART FORMS

This pop-up technique is simi-lar to the multi-slit mechanism (see p. 56). Here, however, you cut out separate planes and attach them parallel to the base planes. It is one of the simplest tech-niques used in the earliest pop-up books. Provided each layer forms a parallelo-gram, multiple layers enable you to create images of great depth. Theoretically, you could use any number of layers; in practice you are restricted by the amount of paper that enables comfortable closure of the card.

Make sure your base is wide enough to hide the mechanism when the card is closed or it will spoil the surprise on opening. A multilayered pop-up is designed to be viewed when the two base planes are at 90°, that is to say, the base would form a floor and a back wall. If you want to view a design from a different angle, turn the base 90° to form a back and a side wall. When you have successfully completed this project, try designing one with twice the number of layers and cutouts.

Using a see-through pop-up layer •

Drawing up parallelograms to form layers •

Creating depth using multiple layers •

Hiding the mechanism •

The cut-out animal makes this simple pop-up mechanism appear more intricate, and a see-through pop-up cage further enhances the effect.

TEMPLATES

The lion templates are actual size and need several pieces of differently colored cardboard, which are assembled before mounting. The cage is a straight-forward three-fold construction from a single sheet of cardboard.

Cage

Face

Eyes

Whiskers

Mouth

Accordion head support

Mane

Nose

Tail

Body

Lion support

CONSTRUCTION

When the card is opened, the cage pops up to reveal a lion whose head is attached to its body by accordion folded tabs. These keep the head projecting from the body and give the lion added dimension.

Lion support

Cage

Lion base

Base

71

1 *Trace all the lion templates and transfer them onto thin cardboard: orange for the body and head, and brown for the mane. Cut them out and put them aside.*

2 *Trace and transfer onto the same thin cardboard the two accordion head supports. Cut them out, score and fold them. Flatten the folds with a straight edge.*

3 *Assemble the lion's head, gluing the mane, eyes, nose, mouth, and whiskers. Spear small features with a craft knife point and apply glue with a toothpick before lowering them carefully into position.*

4 *Paste the plume to the tip of the tail. Then apply glue to one end of each of the accordion head supports and attach them to the body.*

5 *Glue the other two ends of the head supports and fix the head firmly in place.*

6 *Choose a piece of cardboard that contrasts well with the lion and cage, and fold it in half. Cut out, score and fold the lion support, using the same color as the card itself to make it inconspicuous. The support should be two thirds of the height of the lion's body. Glue one tab of the lion support up to the card fold and hold it in place for a few seconds.*

7 *Fold down the tab at the other end, then apply glue to it. Close the card firmly.*

8 *When you open the card the lion support should pop up. You can now attach the lion to the support. Glue the support first and press the lion to it, making sure that the animal's feet touch the base when the card is open at 90°.*

9 *After measuring and drawing the cage on light gray medium-weight cardboard, cut out the bars, score the folds, and pull them up against a straight edge to fold them without creasing.*

10 *Attach the cage in the same way as the lion support. Remember to glue the cage bottom to the base at the same distance from the fold as the depth of the cage.*

11 *Fold back the cage top and apply a strip of glue along it. While holding the cage down, close the card and keep pressure on it for a few seconds until the glue adheres.*

12 *When the card is opened at right angles, the lion and the cage should be parallel to the back and the base.*

Origami

Origami, from *ori* (to fold) and *kami* or *gami* (paper), is the Japanese art of paper folding. Traditionally the paper may only be folded to the desired shape without cutting, gluing, or any form of added decoration. Therefore, origami designs tend to be geometric and do not produce the organic shapes possible with paper sculpture or papier mâché. They do, however, possess the serene simplicity common to many forms of Japanese art.

From our early schooldays we can probably all remember bringing home a folded paper creation formed from a square of colored paper. Adults also find paper folding a relaxing and fascinating pastime. There is a limited number of basic folds to master, and once you are proficient at these, there is virtually no limit to the designs you can create from a single sheet of paper.

Japanese designs generally use paper that is colored on one side and white on the other. But any paper that creases well is suitable for origami. Practice on photocopy or writing papers and save your good paper for the finished design.

Precision is the main prerequisite for successful origami. Make sure your paper is perfectly square, and use firm pressure when creasing to flatten the folds. It will usually take a couple of attempts to produce satisfactory results, so don't be disheartened by your first try. You can practice origami almost anywhere, with a minimum of materials and space, and most designs can be flattened and stored for future reference.

TWO-COLOR IMAGE

The fox is made from a square of paper that is white on one side and brown on the other. It was carefully folded to make maximum use of the paper and the possibilities presented by the two colors. (Fox, Paul Jackson).

CLEVER CREASING

This cheerful locomotive and cars are made of strong wrapping paper, carefully creased into squares. The wheels are created by pleating and tucking (Locomotive, Max Hulme).

CRAFTY CONTAINERS

You can make your own original boxes and bags using origami paper and techniques. Here, the combination of brightly colored papers and unusual designs results in boxes to treasure rather than discard (Gwynne Radcliffe).

ANIMAL ANTICS

Animals are favorite origami subjects. The two little mice and the sturdy brown bear show what can be achieved. (Mice and Bear, Edwin Corrie).

TYPES OF PAPER

Try to find paper that is fairly thin but reasonably strong so that it does not tear easily. Most origami designs start from squares, and if you are cutting your own paper it is important that this is done accurately. Toy stores and craft stores often sell brightly colored origami paper that has been specially pre-cut into squares (not to be confused with gummed paper squares, which do not fold well), but many types of ordinary paper are also suitable for folding, for example, photocopy paper and plain or patterned gift wrap. The important thing is that the paper must be able to accept and hold a crease; softer types of paper (for example, newspaper) will not hold a crease well.

Valley Fold

The valley fold is the basic origami fold. Everything you make will involve this type of crease. For the symbol for a valley fold and other origami symbols, see page 53.

1 *With the right side of the paper face up, lift one corner of the paper and form a sharp crease.*

2 *Viewed from the right side. If both sides are raised, the crease resembles a valley.*

Mountain Fold

A mountain fold is the counterpart of the valley fold. Because it is difficult to bend paper underneath itself, it is easier to turn the paper over and form a valley fold. Remember to reverse the paper after you have made the fold.

1 *With the wrong side face up, fold over the paper and form a sharp crease.*

2 *Viewed from the right side, the crease forms a distinctive ridge.*

Inside Reverse Fold

The reverse fold is very useful, as it can be adapted to a number of different shapes. This is a triangular shape, formed with a diagonal fold, but you can start with any shape of fold.

1 *Fold your sheet of paper in half diagonally. Pull one corner toward you.*

2 *Form a sharp crease along the corner and then open up the crease.*

3 *Pinching the center of the paper with your left hand, grip the right-hand corner and pull down.*

4 *Tuck the corner inside the main fold and crease firmly.*

5 *All of the creases that make up the inside reverse fold can be seen here.*

Outside Reverse Fold

The difference between an inside reverse and an outside reverse fold is that in an inside fold the part of the paper that moves is reversed inside the paper, and in an outside fold it is reversed outside the paper.

1 *Fold your sheet of paper in half. Press one corner up, away from you.*

2 *Form the crease firmly and then open out the fold.*

3 *Holding the piece of paper open with your left hand, grip the corner with your right hand.*

4 *Press the corner back so that the wrong side of the paper is revealed, then press the creases firmly.*

5 *When the paper is opened out, you can see that the corner folds have changed from mountain to valley folds.*

Squash Fold

The squash fold involves the simultaneous creation of several creases. Although more demanding than the other basic folds, it occurs frequently in origami, so it is a useful fold to master.

1 *Fold your paper in half diagonally and fold one corner away from you.*

2 *Form the crease firmly and then insert your finger into the fold.*

3 *Using the fingers of your other hand, press the fold back on itself.*

4 *Crease the folds formed by the action in step 3.*

5 *Here you can see the various creases that form the squash fold.*

Windmill Base

The windmill base is an interesting form. It can be adapted by forming only some of the "sails" into a variety of shapes.

1 *Fold your paper in half horizontally in both directions and then diagonally in both directions.*

2 *Open all folds except the last one. Fold each edge to the center, opening up after each fold.*

3 *Looking at the back, you can see the complex web of mountain and valley folds that you have formed.*

4 *Turn the paper over. Fold in one corner to the center.*

5 *Repeat for all four corners, making sure your folds are clean and accurate.*

6 *Open up the folds and turn the paper over. Press down gently on the four points of the inner square.*

7 *The corners will pop up. Lifting from below, collapse the corners onto the center square.*

8 *Flatten one corner down on itself, creating a squash fold.*

9 *Repeat for all four corners, so that you have a flat square.*

10 *Turn one of the squash folds outward, so that the point sticks out beyond the square.*

11 *Repeat for the other three squash folds to form the windmill shape.*

Fish Base

The fish base is also known as the kite base. The basic outline shape is very simple, but further folds create a more complex structure that is more adapted for developing other shapes.

1 Fold the paper in half diagonally. Open up. Fold the right-hand corner into the center.

2 Fold the left-hand corner in and turn the paper over.

3 Fold the bottom point up to meet the top point. Press the crease firmly.

4 Turn the paper over toward you.

5 Insert your finger in the top of the left flap and lift, creating a squash fold and a petal fold.

6 Pull out the point and crease in place.

7 Repeat on the right-hand crease.

Envelope

ART
FORMS

To give your letters a personal touch, you can create your own envelopes using origami. The stylish design shown here is both elegant and practical. The sharp folds and points give the envelope a geometric feel, emphasized by the use of two-colored paper.

Some of the actions are tricky to achieve because you must manipulate several folds at once, but with practice they are easily mastered. Try them out on some scrap paper before starting on the project. The locking device inside the flap is an interesting feature: it is invisible and yet it

- **Manipulating several folds at once**
- **Incorporating strengthening folds**
- **Using two-colored paper**

holds the point of the flap together and strengthens the whole structure of the envelope.

This project uses three of the basic origami folds — valley fold, mountain fold, and squash fold. It is important to practice these folds until you have mastered them as they form the basis for many origami projects.

This striking two-tone envelope will complement a handmade card to perfection, or add a touch of distinction to a letter for a special recipient.

1 *Take a piece of paper 15 in. (38 cm) square. With the wrong side face up, fold in half. Repeat.*

2 *Make diagonal folds to check that the paper is square.*

3 *Fold in the bottom edge to the center crease as shown.*

4 *Rotate the paper 180° and repeat on the opposite edge.*

5 *Turn the paper over to reveal the mountain fold.*

6 *Fold the bottom right-hand corner over to the center crease.*

7 *Repeat this on the right-hand crease.*

8 *Turn the paper over. The corners are now tucked under to form a point, and the folded edges are revealed.*

9 *Turn the paper so that the point is toward you. Fold over the point, forming the crease to meet the corners of the point.*

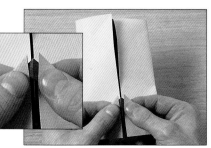

10 *Hold either side of the point between your thumb and forefinger.*

11 *Gripping only the outer fold, pull both sides outward.*

12 *Use your other fingers to tuck in the folds behind the points. This should be carried out in one swift action.*

13 Press down the crease and make sure that the inner and outer edges of the points align neatly.

14 Insert your finger into the right-hand corner.

15 Press the squash fold into place.

16 Press down the creases. The inner fold has changed from a valley fold to a mountain fold.

17 Repeat the squash fold on the left-hand point.

18 Insert a thumb under each of the center corner flaps and lift.

19 Grip each corner between a thumb and forefinger.

20 Pull each corner outward.

21 Change the position of your fingers and press the upper flaps down.

22 Press the corners into position.

23 Make sure that all edges line up.

24 Lift the left-hand flap.

25 *Mountain fold the two corners to form a point.*

26 *Fold the point back firmly.*

27 *Repeat to make a point on the right-hand flap.*

28 *To make the flap, fold the top right-hand corner down along the center line.*

29 *Repeat for the left-hand corner.*

30 *To make the locking device, hold the left-hand corner and grip the tip of the inner fold.*

31 *Pull the inner point out so that it forms a tab.*

32 *Press the inner tab inside the flap to flatten and define the creases.*

33 *Tuck the tab under the right-hand flap as shown.*

34 *Repeat to make the right-hand tab and tuck that under the left-hand flap.*

35 *The tabs are now invisible, but the flap of the envelope is much stronger.*

36 *Fold the flap down and tuck it into place.*

Gift Boxes and Brooch

ART FORMS

This project is a variation on a theme that has been popular for centuries, especially in Russia, where peasants used to carve wooden dolls in decreasing sizes that split open and fitted inside each other. Each set could be made up of as many as 12 dolls. This project consists of three nesting boxes, but you could make as many as you wanted.

When presenting the boxes as a gift to someone, what could be nicer than including an extra surprise present in the inner box? Follow the instructions given on page 87 for an attractive brooch. In order to demonstrate clearly the detailed folds, the brooch is made in a larger format. To fit the brooch inside the smallest box, start with a piece of paper 4¾ x 4¾ in. (12 x 12cm) square. You can purchase a brooch pin from craft stores to stick on the back.

Repeating sequences of folds •
Creating three-dimensional objects •
Using reinforcing folds for strength •

Everyone enjoys the excitement of opening a box and finding another one nesting within it, opening that and finding yet another box, and then finally reaching the treasure at the heart of the stack. Here, a "jeweled" origami brooch is concealed within three multi-color boxes.

MAKING THE OUTER BOX

1 *Divide your paper into equal thirds by rolling it into place between your fingers as shown.*

2 *Pinch the top of the paper to indicate the position of the thirds.*

3 *Place the paper face down. Using your mark as a guide, fold the left-hand third into the center and crease.*

4 *Open up and repeat the process for the right-hand third.*

5 *Rotate the paper 90° and again divide the paper into thirds.*

6 *Repeat steps 3 and 4 so that you have four intersecting valley folds.*

7 *Fold both sides inward, using your existing crease as a guide.*

8 *Open up the folds to reveal the extra crease as shown.*

9 *Fold the top third of the paper down along the existing crease line.*

10 *Insert the fingers of your left hand under the fold, using your right hand to hold it down.*

11 *Make an internal diagonal crease across the central box in the paper.*

12 *Press the crease firmly into the corner so that the box sides stand up.*

13 Pull up the right-hand corner in the same way.

14 Make a diagonal fold to form a triangle on the base of the box.

15 Make sure that the top edges of the two corners align exactly.

16 Open up the two corners so that your paper is flat once again.

17 Rotate your paper 180° and repeat steps 9–15 to form the last two corners.

18 Refold the corners at the other end along the existing creases.

19 Your box now has four upright sides and a base strengthened by two folded triangles.

20 Lift one of the triangles. Using the tip of the triangle as a guide, fold over the two layers of paper.

21 Fold the adjacent side next, taking the fold line of the first side as guide.

22 Fold down the final two sides and then define all of the corner creases.

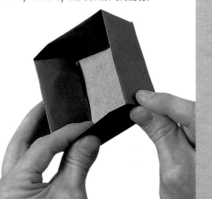

SIZING THE INNER BOXES

Repeat the instructions to make a base and a lid for as many boxes as you require. For each base, your paper should be ¼ in. (5mm) square smaller than the paper used for the lid. The lid of each box should be ½ in. (10mm) square smaller than the next. These are the sizes used for this project:

Outer box
Lid   10 x 10 in. (25 x 25cm)
Base 9¾ x 9¾ in.
      (24.5 x 24.5cm)
Middle box
Lid   9½ x 9½ in. (24 x 24cm)
Base 9¼ x 9¼ in.
      (23.5 x 23.5cm)
Inner box
Lid   9 x 9 in. (23 x 23cm)
Base 8¾ x 8¾ in.
      (22.5 x 22.5cm)

MAKING THE BROOCH

1 To start, complete steps 1–9 of the windmill base (see page 82).

2 Fold the edge of the top right-hand corner into the center crease as shown.

3 Repeat on the other edge and for the other three corners.

4 Holding the points flat in the center, lift up the flaps to the vertical.

5 Squash fold the flap flat.

6 Repeat the squash fold for the other seven flaps.

7 Fold back one of the corners, taking your line from the tips of the flaps.

8 Repeat for the other three corners, then turn the paper over and define the creases.

9 The octagonal shape and geometric folds suggest a simple faceted jewel.

Origami Camel

ART FORMS

Using advanced techniques in combination •

Creating and narrowing free points •

Depicting a living creature •

Origami animals are extremely popular, despite being difficult subjects to depict; their curved forms and enclosed volumes do not readily lend themselves to a craft in which straight edges and flat planes predominate. The creative challenge is to find a way to demonstrate their essential form, rather than the detail, so that the creature can instantly be recognized from a few simple shapes. This essential form is achieved first by creating a number of free points to represent the limbs, head, etc. The fish base used here is an excellent starting shape for designing animals, since it has both sharp and blunt free points.

The tricky part of the design comes at steps 25 and 27. The folds themselves are easy, but need positioning accurately so that the head and neck of the camel are properly proportioned. If your first attempt looks a little malformed, unfold back to step 24 and reposition the creases.

Use a square of thin paper, at least 8 × 8 in. (20 × 20cm). A small dab of glue may be necessary to hold the layers of the hump together. When you have learned to make the camel, try changing the folds to make a giraffe or a llama.

This little group is so atmospheric that you can almost see the sand stretching endlessly beneath the camels' feet. Display them along the top of a bookcase or, to protect them from dust, on a shelf in a glass-fronted cabinet.

1 *First make a fish base using the method described on page 79.*

2 *Separate the two loose corners, pulling them apart.*

3 *Establish a long mountain crease across the middle. The paper remains three-dimensional.*

4 *Gather the layers together. Grip firmly behind the triangles with your left hand.*

5 *Swivel your right hand downward, flattening the projecting triangles to the right.*

6 *Press the paper firmly flat.*

7 *Narrow the nearside triangle.*

8 *Unfold the crease.*

9 *Narrow the spike at the top left. Note the curved pocket that lifts up. Allow it to stand.*

10 *Unfold. Make a short crease. This connects the intersection of the previous two creases with the bottom corner.*

11 *Form all three creases at the same time by collapsing the paper.*

12 *Press firmly.*

13 *Turn the shape over and repeat steps 7–12 on this side of the paper.*

14 *Note how the upper corners are now much narrower than in step 6.*

15 *Pull the layers apart, allowing the sharp spike to dip and flatten.*

16 *The spike is now almost flat. Continue to pull the layers apart.*

17 *Stop pulling when the shape looks like this. Firmly grip the paper at the top and begin to lift the spike.*

18 *Twist the spike out to the right. Flatten and crease.*

19 *Using the same method, twist the spike out to the left and crease.*

20 *Squeeze the spike in half, while folding the remainder of the paper in half.*

21 *Press the paper flat.*

22 *Inside reverse fold (see p.76) the lowest corner along existing creases, to its step 23 position.*

23 *The corner now points to the left. Press the paper flat.*

24 *Flip the paper over so that the two leg points point downward.*

25 *Valley fold the neck spike.*

26 *Unfold and outside reverse (see p.77) the spike along the line of the valley fold.*

27 *Similarly, valley fold again to create the head.*

28 *Outside reverse the spike along the line of the valley fold.*

29 *Pull out the layers inside the spike to make a sturdy head.*

30 *Repeat the process on the far side of the spike.*

31 *This is the view of the top of the camel. Fold the tip of the spike inside the head.*

32 *Hold the nose as shown, pulling the layers apart.*

33 *Turn the front edge back on itself to create a thick ridge across the nose.*

34 *The head is now complete. Some of the creases may need repositioning.*

35 *Valley fold the rear leg, as shown.*

36 *Unfold, then outside reverse the leg along the line of the valley fold.*

Weaving

Woven paper is an ancient art form that probably originated in Asia. With all of the wonderful papers available today, you can create beautiful designs to frame, or use as greeting cards, bookmarks, table mats, book covers, and picture mounts.

Weaving is done by threading the weft (horizontal) strips over and under the warp (vertical) strips. Practice a simple weave of two colored strips before attempting an irregular pattern of over-and-under permutations using contrasting colors or different textures. Try making handmade papers from vegetation and recycled paper (see p. 124). Then weave them together in interesting colors and texture combinations to form a geometric design with a beautiful organic quality. Experiment with a variety of weaves, and develop adaptations of your own. Make a three-dimensional weave by creasing some of the warp and weft to create parts that stand out from the rest. Combine this with intricate weaves to create more wonderfully complex designs. Use two identical photographs, or wrapping paper with bold geometric designs, and weave the strips slightly out of alignment to achieve intriguing, double-take effects.

TOOLS AND MATERIALS

- ✓ Metal ruler
- ✓ Protractor
- ✓ Triangle
- ✓ Craft knife
- ✓ Pencil
- ✓ Glue
- ✓ Scissors
- ✓ Cutting mat
- ✓ Photographs
- ✓ Clippings
- ✓ Adhesive plastic film
- ✓ Papers in different colors and weights

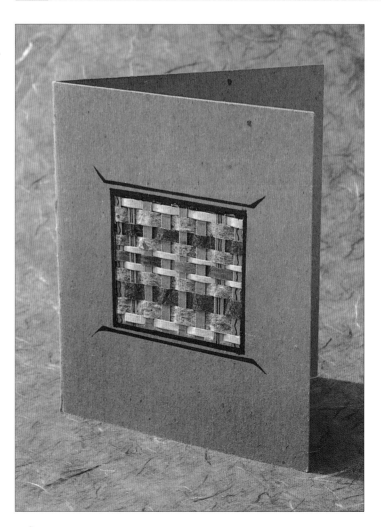

NATURAL PAPERS
The combination of recycled papers, earth colors, and a simple woven pattern makes a striking greeting card (Jo Carlill).

BEAUTIFUL BASKETS

Woven paper is very durable and, as seen here, looks like fabric when woven into baskets (Mary Butcher).

WARP

WEFT

The warp defines the vertical strands of the weave. You can cut them from the same piece of paper, leaving them attached at the top for ease of handling.

The weft describes the horizontal strands. These are intertwined through the warp. Each weft strand alternates its starting point from the one above.

WASTEPAPER BASKET

Bright paper strips in various widths were woven into this basket. The band at the top was loosely sewn around the rim as a finishing touch (Mary Butcher).

Plain Weave

Interweaving paper allows you to create some striking designs. Yet, it is one of the simplest of the paper art forms. The "under and over" plain weave is the best one to start with. The pattern repeats every two rows and appears staggered, much like brickwork. You can create some interesting variations by varying the width of the warp (vertical) and weft (horizontal) strips, or using paper with a deckle edge to soften the hard edges.

1 *Take a piece of medium-weight paper 4 × 3¾ in. (100 × 95mm) wide. Make four vertical cuts ¾ in. (19mm) apart, leaving the top ¼ in. (6mm) intact. Cut five pieces 6 × ¾ in. (152 × 19mm) in a different color for the weft strips.*

2 *Starting at the top, weave the first weft strip through the warp, over the first, under the second, over the third and so on to the last warp.*

3 *Take the second weft strip and weave it under the first warp strip, over the second, and so on. Alternate the procedure for the first and second strips for the remaining weft strips.*

4 *Make sure you push each weft up to the previous one, keeping your weave straight and tight. You can either glue each strip in position as you work, putting a dab of glue at each end, or wait until all the strips are in position.*

5 *When the strips are firmly glued, trim the edges, and finally the ¼ in. (6mm) top. Glue the remaining strips along the top edge.*

USING COLORED PAPER AND TEXTURE

Many interesting weaves can be created using the innate qualities of the paper. Choose different textures in a single color for subtle patterns, or exploit the myriad of colored papers for eye-catching effects. Utilize old letters, maps, manuscripts, wrapping papers, and hand-colored sheets — experimentation is part of the fun.

Different textures

Three different colors

Irregular Weave

Some weaves work best with two colors while others work well with three or four colors. Irregular weaves are mathematical variations of the plain weave and the permutations are endless. Some well-known ones are the zig-zag, the patchwork, and the shadow blocks weave. The patchwork is an irregular weave that works well using three or four different colored papers.

1 Cut your pieces as you did for the plain weave, this time using eight strips ³⁄₈ in. (8mm) wide.

2 Weave the second weft under one warp, over one, under one and so on to the end of the row.

3 Weave the third weft under two warps, then over two warps, and so on. Be sure to keep the strips tight.

4 Weave the fourth weft over one warp, under one, over one and so on to the end of the row.

5 Start again at step 1 and repeat this sequence until the weave is complete. Glue and trim as for the plain weave.

Old manuscript

Wrapping paper

Marbled paper

3-D Weave

Unique and unusual wallhangings can be created by using a 3-D weave. By adding folds to the warp and the weft they project from the surface of the flat weave. If you hang the weaving opposite a natural light source the projections cast interesting shadows that change as the sun moves across the sky.

1 Cut a piece of yellow paper 9 × 6 in. (228 × 152mm) wide. Make seven vertical cuts to create eight warp strips ¾ in. (19mm) wide. Leave ½ in. (13mm) intact at the top. Cut eight green weft strips ¾ × 9 in. (19 × 230mm) long.

2 Weave the second strip from the left side, folding it back after the sixth warp strip. Crease the fold with your finger.

3 Curl the green strip back on itself, creating a fold that touches the left side of the warp strip. Then fold it back the opposite way, so that you have two valley folds and one mountain fold ¾ in. (19mm) apart.

4 Weave the end of the weft strip over the seventh and under the eighth warp, leaving the folded weft projecting from the surface of the weave.

5 Fold the second warp strip upward and crease. Then fold it back to repeat the complete procedure in step 3, ending with a mountain projection in the warp.

6 Continue weaving from left to right, as in step 2, but this time folding the strip back after the fifth warp. Repeat step 3. Then fold the third warp strip up and create a mountain projection.

7 Continue making projections that converge toward the center, as shown, up to the fourth weft strip. Reverse the entire procedure from the fifth to the eighth wefts.

8 Check that all of the projections are standing up before gluing the loose ends. Trim the woven edges and the top ½ in. (13mm).

Tumbling Blocks Weave

Begin with an orange warp 6½ × 4½ in. (165 × 114mm) wide. Cut six vertical strips in it ¾ in. (19mm) wide. Cut six yellow weft strips ¾ × 6 in. (19 × 152mm) long, and weave from the right. **Row 1** *over 1, under 1, over 2, under 1, over 1.* **Row 2** *over 2, under 1, over 2, under 1.* **Row 3** *under 1, over 2, under 1, over 2.* **Row 4, 5,** *and* **6** *are repetitions of rows 1, 2, and 3.*

1 *Make eight red strips ½ × 6 in. (13 × 152mm) long. Fold one end of each strip to a point so that it will be easier to weave.*

2 *Beginning at the top left corner, weave a red strip over the first warp and under the second weft. Hold the main weave together as you work.*

3 *Turn the weave over and weave the second strip under the third warp from the right to emerge between the second warp and third weft.*

4 *Continue weaving strips from the top to form a gradually evolving pattern of blocks. Proceed to the bottom right corner. Keep turning your work over to pull ends through.*

5 *Glue and trim all of the edges to complete a three-dimensional effect.*

BOOKMARKS

Intricate weaves using narrow strips of paper make beautiful bookmarks. Choose a rainbow of colors, an earthy-toned handmade paper interwoven with the pages of a discarded paperback, or some marbled paper that calls to mind the end papers of an old book. Protect your bookmarks with adhesive plastic film (available in craft stores).

Connect paper shapes by weaving them together with long narrow strips. Or weave a variety of papers through evenly placed slits. Design your own version and include it when giving a book as a present.

Book Cover

ART FORMS

Applying imagery and color to a theme •

Designing a cut-out shape to fit an object •

A woven book cover can reflect the contents of the volume in more than just design. An atlas cover could combine pictures of sea and land or it could consist of interwoven maps. Weave together seed packets to cover a gardening guide, or old music sheets for a piano book. Make a montage of memorable photographs and handmade papers to decorate the family album. Wildlife books look striking when covered in enlarged interwoven details of animal coats: zebra, tiger, and giraffe skins, or peacock feathers, for example. Again consider the possibility of varying the widths of the strips or incorporating papers with a deckle edge. Use some of the papers that you have marbled, spattered, or sponged (see p.46). Covering the weave with adhesive plastic film will keep it clean however well-thumbed the book.

A treasured book needs protection, and what could be more suitable than a cover of your own design to reflect the contents or enhance your decor? Make a bookmark to match for a perfect gift set.

TEMPLATE

Since books differ in size, we cannot give measurements, but the principle is the same for all. Place the opened book on a sheet of paper. Mark the rectangle formed by the book cover and add the tabs to it as shown.

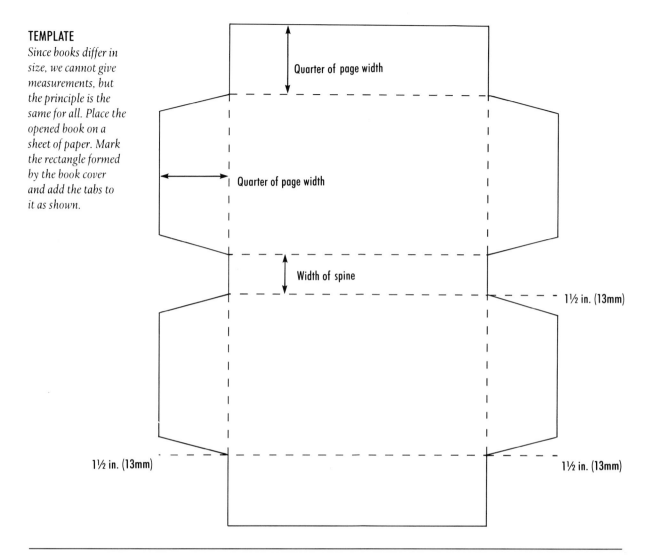

Quarter of page width

Quarter of page width

Width of spine

1½ in. (13mm)

1½ in. (13mm)

1½ in. (13mm)

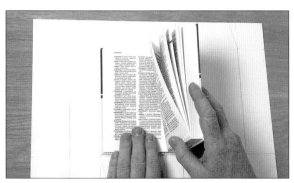

1 *Return the book to the outlined paper and check that it fits before trimming.*

2 *Cut horizontal slits in the book cover. These will form the weft strips. It is up to you and the size of your book how wide you make the strips.*

3 *Turn the corner over and measure and mark the warp strips as shown.*

4 *Cut out warp strips to correspond. Here, we used ⅝ in. (15mm) wide strips.*

5 *Beginning at the top left, weave the warp down through the weft to create a pattern of your choice. Here, a crossword design is being made. Row 1: under 2, over 2, under 2, over 2, and so on until you reach the end.*

6 *Row 2: over 3, under 1, over 3, under 1, repeat to the end.*

7 *Row 3: over 1, under 2, over 2, under 2, and so on to the end. Turn the piece over and then butt the strips together to tighten the weave.*

8 *Row 4: under 1, over 1, under 1, over 1. Repeat the pattern to the end, tightening the weave after each strip is added.*

9 *Repeat these four weaving sequences until you reach the right-hand side of your cover.*

10 *It is impossible to butt the strips without leaving a little space, so you might find the last strip difficult to fit. In this case, trim a sliver from it.*

11 *If the strip still sticks, widen the slit by about $^1/_{16}$ in. (1mm), or just enough to accommodate it.*

12 *Weave the strip through, pulling gently rather than pushing to avoid catching.*

13 *Score the pencil lines along the tabs. Then turn the paper over, fold up as shown, and flatten the folds.*

14 *Open the folds and place the book on the cover. Fold up the tabs on the left-hand cover to enclose the book. Repeat on the right-hand cover, and close the book, making sure that the cover fits snugly.*

Greeting Card

project
8

Designing greeting cards •

Creating impact with a minimal design •

ART
FORMS

Making your own greeting card has a number of advantages. Whatever the occasion, a homemade card carries more meaning than a store-bought card and can become a unique keepsake for the recipient. And, a handmade card is always special, indicating that you cared enough to spend time and thought on creating something unique.

In Japan many people make their own cards, decorating them with a sketch, brushwork, woodblock print, or stamped image. Paper is a tactile material: the shape, color, and texture of a card made with handmade organic papers appeal to the eye and touch. Use paper made with flowers from your yard, and even perfume them, if you wish, before you weave them. Or copy a letter that your friend has sent you, and combine it with handmade papers. Vary color and texture to suit the occasion and the message; the qualities of the materials go a long way in conveying your sentiments. Write your greeting neatly, without flourishes: let your design speak for itself.

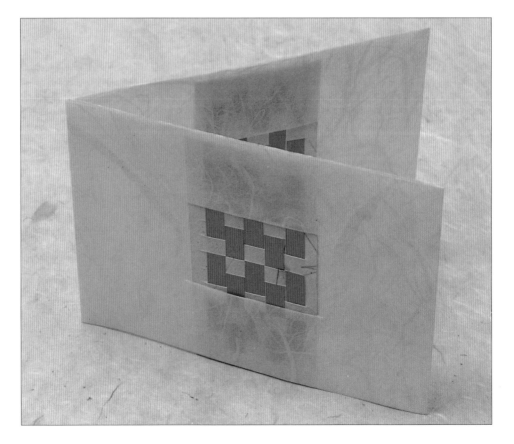

This design illustrates a two-stage weave: small strips are woven through a larger strip, and that strip is woven into the card.

1 Take a piece of semi-translucent paper, such as Japanese handmade paper, 5 × 20 in. (127 × 508mm) long. Fold it in half, open it, and fold each end into the center.

2 Measure and cut a 1¾ × 3½ in. (44 × 89mm) rectangle of paper, and make a series of 13 slits, 1¼ in. (32mm) wide, across its width as shown.

3 Cut five colored paper strips ¼ × 4 in. (6 × 100mm) long. Use the five to create an irregular weave as shown. Repeat the process with strips of a contrasting color.

4 If you want the depth of the card and the woven strip to be the same, position the strip on the card and trim the excess.

5 Make two slits through the four thicknesses of the card in the center, 1¾ in. (44mm) wide and 1¾ in. (44mm) apart.

6 Slot one woven strip through the front two thicknesses of the card, and the other through the back two thicknesses. The result is a beautifully simple card that relies on the color and texture of the paper for its design.

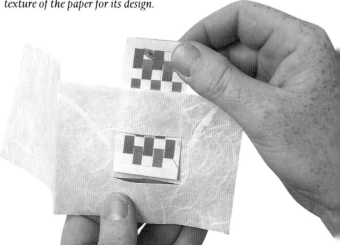

Collage

Collage is the art of juxtaposing photographs, pieces of paper, and found objects and gluing them to a surface as elements of a picture. The name comes from the French verb *coller*, to paste.

Decoupage is a form of collage. The name comes from the French word for "cut out." This art, which was developed at the French court in the 18th century, consists of cutting out printed paper images, gluing them to boxes or furniture, and varnishing them to produce an inlaid effect. To achieve a lacquered effect, you need to apply about 10 to 15 coats of varnish, which makes it quite a time-consuming task.

Although collages were being made as far back as the 12th century, it is generally agreed that the French painter Georges Braque invented collage as we think of it today. Around 1910, both he and Pablo Picasso were experimenting with collage as a new artistic technique. They were soon followed by Henri Matisse who created a series of stunningly simple abstracts from brightly colored, apparently random paper shapes glued to white backgrounds.

You can use a vast variety of papers in collage, ranging from commercial or handmade papers to recycled papers such as newspaper clippings, postage stamps, and bus tickets. Start to build up a collection, paying attention to colors and textures. The most suitable adhesives for collage are polyvinyl acetate and wallpaper paste, which can be thinned with water.

TOOLS AND MATERIALS

- ✔ 2 in. (5 cm) paint brush
- ✔ 1 in. (2.5 cm) paint brush
- ✔ Polyvinyl acetate glue
- ✔ Wallpaper paste
- ✔ Plastic sheeting
- ✔ Ruler
- ✔ Pencil
- ✔ Scissors
- ✔ Craft knife
- ✔ Papers in a variety of colors
- ✔ Magazine clippings
- ✔ Postcards
- ✔ Music manuscript
- ✔ Wallpapers
- ✔ Gift wrapping and tags
- ✔ Varnish

COLOR MOSAIC
*This colorful composition was created by cutting out each shape and adding it to the work in a particular order; starting with the background and building up to the foreground to create a vivid impact (*Flowerscope, *Karen Pathau).*

USING UNUSUAL PAPERS
The artist created a textural collage composition using watercolor on pieces of torn Japanese paper. The long fibers in the paper give the torn paper an extra rough edge (One of the "Golden Series" of paperworks, Joanne Soroka).

MIXED MEDIA
Layers of torn and cut paper have been combined with monoprint, gold paint, and white pastel to create a richly textured work. The papers used include recycled chocolate and candy wrappers. (Sun Worshippers, Mary Chapman).

Overlapping Cut Paper

This technique is very useful for increasing the number of colors you can include in a composition. By overlapping sections of paper, you can combine the colors to create new ones. This technique only works with thin papers such as tissue paper.

1 *Cut strips of paper from different colored tissue paper. Choose light and dark shades for maximum effect. Arrange these in place on a piece of watercolor paper.*

2 *Once you are happy with your arrangement, glue the back of each piece of tissue paper and stick it in place. Here you can see the difference between the colors achieved by placing yellow on red, and red on yellow.*

Overlapping Torn Paper

Cut shapes have hard edges. If you want a more muted effect, tear your shapes rather than cut them. The ragged edge will soften the merging of the two colors, and a subtle gradation of tone can be achieved.

1 *Tear out a variety of shapes in tissue paper in a number of different colors. The more ragged the torn edge, the better, so try to tear with and against the grain for variety.*

2 *Lay out your pieces on watercolor paper and try out various arrangements. Here several strips are placed close to one another, creating a rainbow effect.*

3 *When you are happy with your arrangement, apply glue to the back of each paper shape and stick it in place.*

4 *Flatten out creases with your hand as you go, but remember to handle the tissue paper carefully; it is delicate and will tear or stretch easily.*

5 *The finished composition suggests a sunset over water. The subtle effects created by this technique are useful for natural subjects such as landscapes.*

Crumpling

Sometimes it is useful to be able to introduce texture into a composition. This can be done by crumpling the pieces before applying them to the paper. Combined with gluing of selected areas, crumpling can also be used to create specific structure.

1 *Tear out your pieces and apply some of them flat onto the paper. This composition is of oranges. Select one of the orange shapes and crumple it with your fingers.*

2 *Glue the back of the crumpled orange and press it into place, taking care not to flatten the creases. Add more oranges, combining crumpled and flat ones.*

3 *Cut out a leaf shape and crumple it. Using a tube of glue for better control, draw a line in glue on the back to represent the vein.*

4 *Press the leaf into place along the glue line. The creases will lift the leaf away from the paper, enhancing the effect of the vein.*

5 *Add more leaves. As the glue dries, the creases will be pulled in toward the vein line, emphasizing the leaf structure.*

GLUING TIPS

When working with paper there are several different adhesives you can use, including polyvinyl acetate (PVA), clear household cement in a tube, glue sticks, and glue pens. This chart shows the recommended applications of the main types of adhesive and the art forms they can be used for. Checks indicate suitability, crosses indicate lack of suitability.

TYPE OF GLUE	Heavy	Medium	Light	ART FORMS
Glue sticks	✗	✗	✔	Collage, Origami, Weaving
Glue pens	✗	✗	✔	Collage, Origami, Weaving
Clear glue	✔	✔	✔	Paper Sculpture, Pop-ups
PVA	✔	✔	✗	Paper Sculpture, Papier Mâché, Collage, Pop-ups
Wallpaper paste	✗	✗	✔	Papier Mâché, Collage
Rubber cement	✗	✔	✔	Paper Sculpture, Weaving, Pop-ups, Paper Cuts, Collage
Silicone sealant	✔	✔	✔	Paper Sculpture

Tulips

ART
FORMS

This charming picture of tulips is laid on an unusual background. An effect like this is created by weaving strips of tissue paper. The texture is far more interesting than that created by using flat layers of paper. All the elements made from tissue paper were torn rather than cut. This gives a soft effect and contrasts well with the harder, crisper edge of the flowers themselves. These were cut from magazine pages, and appropriate colors were chosen to represent the petals and the leaves.

Fabric paint was used to outline the tulips and also to draw in the shape of the petals. This serves to highlight the main subject of the composition and add detail. Fabric paints are also useful when you need to neaten rough edges.

You can outline the flowers, stem and leaves with dimensional fabric paint. Finally, you can protect this delicate piece by mounting and framing it. A ready made clip frame is an inexpensive, easy option, or you can have it framed professionally.

1 Tear out a rectangle from dark blue tissue paper. It should be 12 in. (30cm) long and 6 in. (15cm) wide. Glue it onto a piece of white watercolor paper.

2 Using a metal rule as a hard edge to tear against, tear off 12 strips approximately ½ in. (1.5cm) wide from a sheet of light blue tissue paper 10 in. (25cm) long. Then tear 16 strips from a sheet 5 in. (12.5cm) long.

3 Place all the long strips side by side. Place the metal rule across the center of the strips and flip over alternate strips. Place one of the shorter strips parallel with the rule.

4 Lift the metal rule carefully at both ends. Twist it away from you slowly so that the long strips fall back in place. They should overlap the short strip.

5 Repeat this action, butting the next short strip close to the first one. Continue in this way until you reach the end of the long strips, then rotate your work and start to work out from the center again.

6 Once all the strips have been interwoven, glue the loose ends in place. Use only a drop of glue applied with a small wooden skewer.

7 Allow the glue to dry. Then trim your work by placing the metal rule along the outside strip on each edge and tearing off the loose ends.

8 Divide the woven rectangle in half by carefully tearing all the long strips between two of the short strips. Glue the two pieces in place on top of the dark blue background.

9 Cut out flower shapes from magazine pages. When you are happy with the position, glue the back of each piece and stick it down.

Tropical Reef Lampshade

ART FORMS

Personalizing a household item •

Embellishing with beads and sequins •

Repeating a motif •

Collage is such a versatile art form that it is ideal for customizing objects around your home. The designs can be as focused or as abstract as you wish. Single-subject images are suitable for individual items such as boxes or trays. Or you could link several pieces of furniture, such as wooden chairs, by using the same theme to decorate each one.

For this project we have repeated a motif. The circular structure of a lampshade makes a perfect background for an underwater scene. The fish appear to be swimming round and round. When decorating a lampshade, it is better to choose a paper one rather than a fabric one because it will be more in keeping with the paper applied to it. The one used here is parchment. Whatever shade you choose, it is vital to make sure that the shade is fire retardant.

When the light is switched on this collaged fish lampshade glows with all the color and movement of a tropical reef.

MAKING A LAMPSHADE

You can use the same basic method to make a paper lampshade regardless of the size and shape of the frame. Most papers – from newsprint to wallpaper – are suitable, but some will look more effective when the light shines through them.

1 *Mark a starting point with pencil on the frame and then roll it across the paper, tracing the top and bottom as shown. Allow a ¼ in. (6mm) overlap.*

2 *Join the lines at each end with a ruler. Cut out. Check the fit. Glue the edges and paperclip until dry. Apply clear glue to the frame rims, insert frame, and press into place.*

1 To represent the sea, cut lots of small strips from various shades of blue tissue paper. In order to speed up the process, fold your sheet of paper over and cut through several thicknesses at once.

2 Working on a piece of scrap paper, apply glue to the back of each strip and then stick it in place along the bottom of the shade. Overlap some of the strips.

3 Draw a fish shape on thin card. Cut it out and use it as your template to draw several fish on handmade recycled paper of various colors. Cut these out using scissors.

4 Make a second, smaller template in the same way. Cut out some small fish.

5 Apply glue to the back of each fish along the edge and stick them in place. Position your fish carefully; once you have glued them in place, you will not be able to move them because the glue will tear the parchment.

6 Cut more fish out of crumpled wrapping paper to add further variety. Overlap some of the fish when you position them on the lampshade so that they appear to be swimming alongside each other.

7 To highlight the eyes of the fish, use small, flat-backed glass crystal beads. Glue these into place using a small wooden skewer.

8 Outline the edge of each of the fish with fabric paint. This will hide the glue line, which would otherwise show through when the light is shining through the shade.

9 As a finishing touch, add clear sequins to suggest air bubbles in the water.

Mosaic Box

Mimicking the style of a tile mosaic •

Transferring difficult shapes •

**ART
FORMS**

This griffin is reminiscent of ancient Peruvian mosaics. The colors have been chosen to reflect this; the earth tones are appropriate ceramic colors.

When you reproduce a mosaic, the first thing you must do is to break your chosen image into separate sections. Each section should represent an individual "tile." But do not get carried away — if you have too many small tiles, you will create problems. The image will lose clarity, and tiny pieces of paper are tricky to work with. Practice by tracing images from magazines and other books and breaking the outline into sections. Remember to leave space between some of the sections to allow the background to show through, as grouting would show between real tiles.

You can buy blank boxes in all kinds of shapes and sizes from craft suppliers. Choose a shape that will complement the image you have in mind.

You can confine your decoration to the lid of your box or continue it around the sides as here. Give the whole thing two or three coats of clear varnish when you have finished to seal the paper and protect the box.

1 Using a 2B pencil, draw your mosaic griffin on tracing paper. Turn the paper over and draw over all of the pencil lines on the reverse side. Then lay the tracing paper right side up on the lid of your box and draw over the lines.

2 Repeat the same process to transfer the sun shapes onto the box. Next, use your traced image to draw the sun pattern onto the back of some gold paper. Cut the individual shapes out using scissors.

3 Glue the back of each gold shape and stick it in place on the box. Use the traced pencil image as a guide for positioning the pieces.

4 To make the griffin, choose which sections you want to make out of brown paper. Transfer those sections only onto the brown paper using the tracing paper outline. Cut the shapes out using scissors and glue them in place.

5 Select sections in turn for each of the other colors or patterns you wish to use. Repeat the same process of transferring the image onto the paper, cutting out the individual shapes, and gluing them to the box.

6 To make the background, start around the outside edge, away from the other images. Cut lots of squares of uniform size, all from the same light-colored paper. Glue the squares in place, close together.

7 As a finishing touch to the griffin, add a tongue. This animates the features and makes the griffin appear even more fearsome.

8 Add as many complete squares to the background as you have space for. Where a square would overlap part of the image, trace the outline of the shape onto tracing paper. Use this outline to transfer the shape onto the background.

9 Cut out the shape and glue it in place. Repeat this process until the background is complete.

Paper Cuts

ART FORMS

Paper cuts are believed to have originated in ancient China, where they were used to decorate houses, but they are common to many other countries, including Japan, Mexico, Poland, Great Britain, and the Netherlands. In the United States, the Amish community, in particular, are known for their bold folk designs.

Unlike collage or decoupage, which normally uses a printed image, paper-cut designs are derived by the artist from sheets of blank colored paper. Sometimes the paper is folded to give a repeat pattern when cut, such as snowflakes made by school children. This method is common in traditional designs, notably in Poland where country people adorn their homes with monochromatic cutouts created with spring shears (similar to small sheep shears). Their designs include flower and animal motifs, and often have religious or superstitious connotations.

In the nineteenth century it was fashionable in the western world to display framed silhouette portraits of the family or of famous figures. These were cut out with scissors while the sitter posed. The Victorians loved paper, using it for valentine greetings, educational toys for their children, such as cut-out theaters, and Christmas garlands.

Paper cuts can be made with scissors or a knife. Each tool produces different effects. Scissors can vary from Polish shears to fine needlework scissors favored by silhouette artists. A knife needs a sharp pointed blade for detail and flowing curves.

Paper cutting is used extensively by graphic artists and illustrators, whose work appears in magazines and travel brochures. Don't forget to clip any interesting examples you see and add them to your scrapbook.

TOOLS AND MATERIALS

- ✓ Pencil
- ✓ Tracing paper
- ✓ Craft knife
- ✓ Masking tape
- ✓ Stylus
- ✓ Small scissors
- ✓ Roller
- ✓ Cutting mat
- ✓ Glue
- ✓ Papers in different colors and weights

LAYERED PAPERCUT
This is a good example of modern papercut art. The artist used a sharp knife to cut out each colored layer, which he then glued to the background (Red-breasted Goose, David Cooke).

INTRICATE PAPERCUT

This extremely intricate pattern dates from 1855. The image reflects Swiss rural and town life. Note the contrast between the well at the top and the water pumps at the bottom.

PATTERNED PAPERCUT

*Black makes an effective background for these surreal figures. The decorated papers mirror the title of the piece (*Earth, Wind, Water, Fire, *Cynthia Gale).*

Transferring a Tracing

For many of the projects in this book you need to transfer a tracing onto the paper you intend to cut out. The finished cutout must face the opposite way from your original drawing, so you can turn it over and it is ready for use. This saves erasing the pencil lines that are then concealed on the reverse.

1 With a 2B pencil draw or trace your image onto medium- or lightweight tracing paper.

2 Place the drawing face down on a sheet of colored paper and attach the corners with masking tape. Use a hard 2H to 6H pencil to go over the drawing, pressing firmly enough to transfer the image onto the colored paper.

3 Release the tape at two corners and pull the tracing paper back to check that the picture is complete. If you have missed part of it, replace the tracing paper and go over the drawing again.

4 Put the colored sheet on a cutting mat and cut out your drawing with a craft knife.

5 Remove the outline shape from the paper and incise any internal detail.

FISH MOBILE

Using the fish image (above) you can make an attractive mobile. Begin by cutting out three fish as described, then find their point of balance by inserting a needle through one of the vertical slits in the body and suspending the fish; at the point of balance, prick a small hole in the dorsal fin with the needle. Thread a piece of fine black thread through each fish, then suspend them from a thin wire or light stick and hang them in front of a window.

Cutting and Folding

By selective cutting you can bring some parts of an image forward and cause others to recede, while keeping the background intact. Shine a light through the completed cutout to give unusual illuminated outlines to the work.

First, transfer your image onto a sheet of paper (see left). Now decide which elements should recede and mark them with a heavier pencil line. These lines will remain uncut.

1 Carefully cut around your image, following the paler pencil lines. The image should remain securely anchored to the paper.

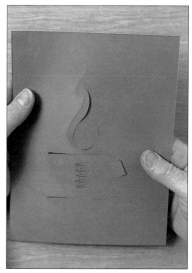

2 Push the sheet from behind to see where adjustments are needed.

3 Ease details forward and backward to create slits of varying size that will allow different amounts of light to penetrate the paper.

4 Shape embossed or scored detail with a stylus or burnisher from the underside. Press firmly.

5 The result is an embossed piece with some cut edges that conveys an interesting soft and hard effect. Shining light through it creates a glowing white outline with graduated color.

Polish Folk Art

Cutting accurately with scissors •

Folding and cutting a repeat pattern •

ART FORMS

In Poland paper-cut designs can be found on tapestries, furniture, and fabric. This traditional folk art was historically carried out by peasant women. Motifs were usually leaves, birds, geometric shapes, and representations of village life, such as harvesting and wedding scenes. Designs, cut from black paper, were usually regional. The Kurpie people, for example, folded their paper twice to produce four identical quarters, and our project is based on their approach.

Although scissors were traditionally used, we suggest a knife for tight corners and details. Use thin paper, which is easy to cut when folded several times, or it will be hard to go into corners without destroying intricate elements. The Polish cut their designs without preliminary drawings, but we advise using a template initially until you gain more confidence. After completing the project, you can devise motifs of your own. An interesting variation, also found in Poland, is multicolored: cut the pattern from black paper and apply one or more colored layers under it.

To make a template, trace a quarter of the design. If you would like to enlarge the design, use a photocopier with an enlargement facility.

1 *Fold a square of black paper in half, then in half again. Use a roller to flatten the folds.*

2 *Transfer the traced image onto the folded square, making sure that the two joined sides of the tracing correspond to the folded sides of the square.*

3 *Carefully cut out the penciled shape, using nail or needlepoint scissors where it is comfortable to do so, and a craft knife for fine detail.*

4 *A craft knife is essential for internal shapes.*

5 *The completed pattern should look like this with all cuts going cleanly through the four thicknesses of paper.*

6 *Open the full-size square with extreme care. There are delicate parts toward the center that can easily rip. Tidy any corners that need it, and your cutout is complete.*

Art Deco Box

Working with colored layer cutouts •
Decorating a 3-D object •

ART FORMS

This project applies the principles of traditional Chinese paper cutting (see p.9) to art deco – the cubist-derived style of the 1920s and 1930s that embraced fine and industrial art. The main image is cut from black paper, color details are applied to the reverse in separate pieces, a sheet in another color is stuck to the back, and the assemblage is mounted onto a cardboard box. The resulting object resembles boxes of the art deco period that were constructed of wood veneers or of silver with an embossed image. It would make an ideal gift in its own right, or could be filled with candies.

Use the same technique to mount the design onto an existing wooden box, and seal it with several coats of varnish in a similar way to de-

coupage (see p.104). Or attach transparent colored paper behind the black paper cutout and hang the finished piece in front of a window like a stained glass plaque so the light can shine through. When selecting an image you will need to consider the shape and size of the object to be decorated. If you find an image which is the right shape but the wrong size, you can enlarge or reduce it on a photocopier with an enlargement facility.

The simple shape and contrasts of this technique are ideally suited to an art deco effect. However, you could achieve very different effects depending on your choice of color and image.

TEMPLATES

Make an enlarged photocopy of these templates to the size you require. Be sure to transfer the color mark-up to your set.

dark flesh

light flesh

SIMPLIFYING AN IMAGE

This technique works well with an image that has strong contrasts. If the image you have chosen has too many subtleties, you can easily simplify it. This papercut was taken from a photo of an art deco stone relief. By placing tracing paper over a photograph you can trace the shadows, thus reducing the image to black and white. Here, color was added to represent flesh tones. Create your own subjects on camera by silhouetting them against the light, or trace high-contrast pictures from magazines.

1 *Trace the black template and transfer it to a piece of thin black paper that is easy to cut.*

2 *Cut out the image, cleanly defining each corner and taking care not to sever any connecting pieces.*

3 *Trace and cut out the dark flesh pieces. Paste them evenly to the back of the black cutout, using dots of glue applied with a toothpick.*

4 *Glue the back of the assembled cutout to a sheet of light flesh colored paper, and press it down firmly with a plastic or rubber roller.*

5 *Turn the piece over to make sure no glue has oozed from the side. Then paste and attach the final dark flesh piece. Check that all parts are securely glued to the light pink sheet.*

6 *Roll the assembled cutout again with a plastic or rubber roller. If any parts are insufficiently adhered, lift them slightly, slide a glued toothpick underneath, and push them into place.*

7 To make the box, take a 9 in. (22.5cm) square of pale blue cardboard (ours is blue on one side and white on the reverse). Draw a line parallel to and 1½ in. (3.75cm) from each edge of the underside. Score the lines.

8 Make two 1½ in. (3.75cm) cuts from the top edge along the penciled line. Repeat on the bottom edge. These will be your glue tabs when you assemble the box lid.

9 Fold all four edges forward to make a box, bringing the blue, or outer, side over the white, or inner, side. Crease the scored lines with your finger, and roll all of the folds.

10 Open the folded lid and place it top side up. Glue the assembled cutout thoroughly on its underside, turn it over, and position it on the blue lid. Center it to leave an even strip of blue all around, and press in place with a roller.

11 Bond the lid by applying two-sided tape to the four corner tabs. Peel away the backing strip and turn the lid over.

12 Fold up the edges and tuck in the corner tabs, pressing them against their neighboring edges to create neat corners. Make another box of the same depth (1½ in./3.75cm) but ⅛ in. (3 mm) shorter to form the base. Fit the lid to the base.

Papermaking

ART FORMS

Paper plays an enormous part in our lives. We use it to record our ideas, package our products, and store the world's knowledge. We turn it into wall coverings and screens, lamp-shades, boxes, and clothes. Yet little thought is given to paper as an art form.

Paper is simple to make and needs little equipment: fiber (from plants, rags, or existing paper); water; a blender or heavy implement for beating the fiber into pulp; a large bowl; pieces of felt or other absorbent material; and two boards. The only special item you need is a mold and deckle — a pair of wooden frames, one of which (the mold) is covered with a mesh screen. The mold and deckle scoops up the pulp and allows it to drain while the sheet is forming. The sheet is then turned out onto a felt-covered board, or couched, before being pressed and dried. You can buy a mold and deckle from a craft supplier, but it is easy to construct your own (see p.126).

Paper consists mainly of cellulose fiber, which is present in all living plants. The most suitable plants for papermaking are those with long cellu-lose fibers that bind to form strong sheets. Hemp and flax are among the best. Cotton rags also make fine paper, because they contain the long, durable fibers of the cotton plant. However, the raw fibers from plants and the processed fibers from cotton rags must first be broken down by prolonged soaking and "cooking" in an alkali solu-tion. A more practical source of papermaking fiber is "half-stuff": partially processed fibers and cloth waste from the textile industry, which can be obtained from papermaking suppliers. Existing papers can also be easily recycled.

Color your paper by making it with colored material, or adding water-soluble dyes to the pulp with an appropriate binder. Incorporate flowers, feathers, and colored threads. Your reward will be a unique paper handmade by a process that is over 2,000 years old.

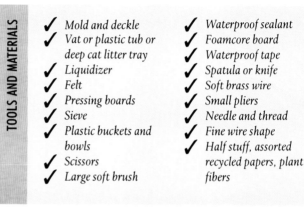

TOOLS AND MATERIALS

- ✓ Mold and deckle
- ✓ Vat or plastic tub or deep cat litter tray
- ✓ Liquidizer
- ✓ Felt
- ✓ Pressing boards
- ✓ Sieve
- ✓ Plastic buckets and bowls
- ✓ Scissors
- ✓ Large soft brush
- ✓ Waterproof sealant
- ✓ Foamcore board
- ✓ Waterproof tape
- ✓ Spatula or knife
- ✓ Soft brass wire
- ✓ Small pliers
- ✓ Needle and thread
- ✓ Fine wire shape
- ✓ Half stuff, assorted recycled papers, plant fibers

COMBINED MEDIA

*The artist skilfully combined colored and layered paper (recycled from an old bible) with machine stitching to create an unusual paper quilt (*Down to Sleep, *Cas Holmes).*

INCORPORATED NATURAL MATERIALS
*This sculptural work combines molded paper with the main constituent that was used to make the paper, namely wood (*Paper and Twigs Sculpture, *S. Benechis).*

LAYERED AND EMBEDDED
*This organic and delicate looking bowl was made by layering paper over a mold and embedding leaves in the layers of paper to achieve a translucent effect (*Large vessel with leaves, *Maureen Hamilton-Hill).*

COLORED PULP
*This colorful piece consists of layered papers that were colored before being pasted onto the blue background (*Dreamer's Stretch, *Akiko Sugiyama).*

Making a mold and deckle

The mold and deckle is the essential tool for papermaking, because it is the device on which the pulp of fiber and water begins to form a sheet of paper. Although referred to and used as a single tool, it consists of two separate wooden frames. These are identical except that the mold is covered with mesh. The pulp drains through the mesh while held in place by the deckle, which defines the shape of the sheet.

1 Take two strips of wood 12 in. (30cm) long and two strips 8 in. (20cm) long × ½–¾ in. (1.25–1.8cm) thick. Pencil a mark ½ in. (1.25cm) from the end of each strip on either side. Cut a groove and chisel out the waste.

2 Assemble the frame, interlocking the chiseled grooves. Glue the joints together with waterproof wood glue. Press them firmly into place, and allow to dry completely.

3 To reinforce the joints, drill a hole and insert a ½ in. (1.25cm) screw in each corner.

4 Seal the screw holes and any gaps in the joints with wood filler, using a craft spatula.

5 Rub the frame with fine sandpaper to remove any roughness, paying special attention to the joints. Then paint it with waterproof varnish to protect it while immersed in the vat.

6 Cut a piece of screen wire to fit the frame and attach it with a staple gun, using stainless steel staples. Staple the corners first so that the screen is evenly stretched.

7 Apply waterproof adhesive tape to seal the edges of the screen and cover the staples. Trim the corners neatly.

8 Repeat steps 1 to 5 to make your deckle. It fits exactly over the mold, ready for use.

Making pulp

The basis of paper is pulp: a semi-liquid mixture of beaten cellulose fiber. Beating causes the fibers to absorb water and unravel. This promotes the bonding that will turn the fibers into paper. Half-stuff, along with other semi-processed textile fibers, and existing papers, are easy to pulp in your kitchen. Soak them in water overnight (or for at least two hours) to loosen the fibers and remove unwanted material.

1 Cut a 4–6 in. (10–15cm) square of half-stuff into strips 1½ in. (3.75cm) wide and then into 1½ in. (3.75cm) squares. Soak in clean water.

2 Place the squares in an electric blender three-quarters full of warm water. Blend thoroughly in two short bursts of 10–15 seconds to obtain a liquidized mixture with evenly distributed fibers.

3 Part-fill the plastic container, or vat, with warm water. You will need about 4 blender goblets of water for each blender of pulp, but be sure to leave a gap of at least 3 in. (7.5cm) at the top of the vat. Pour in the pulp and blend evenly.

4 Recycle scraps of paper to lend color and interest to your pulp. We used postage stamps. Whatever your chosen paper, tear it into small pieces, soak, and liquidize it as you did the half-stuff.

5 Add the recycled pulp to the pulp in the vat and agitate once more to mix. The random effect of the colored paper will be very attractive when the pulp is formed into a sheet.

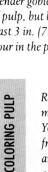

COLORING PULP

Recycled paper is only one means of coloring your pulp. You can use natural dyes – from berries, barks, indigo, and other plant juices – food coloring, water-based paints and inks, textile dyes, or pigments specially designed for coloring pulp. Pigments are available, dry or dispersed in water, from papermaking suppliers and give rich colors. They come with a binder, known as a retention agent, which bonds them to the fibers.

Pigments give clear, vibrant colors. Store pulp in a plastic container covered with a cloth in a cool room.

Forming paper

Forming a sheet of paper calls for a swift, steady hand, but a little practice is all you need to get the hang of it. Try to scoop, lift, and shake the pulp in one smooth action. Before beginning a sheet, stir the pulp gently with your hand to ensure even distribution of the fibers. Left to themselves for more than a few minutes, they constantly gravitate toward the bottom of the container.

1 First wet your mold. Immerse it in water or hold it under a running faucet until it is thoroughly soaked.

2 Place the deckle on top of the mold. Hold the mold and deckle together, with the screen in the middle of the "sandwich," making sure that they are perfectly aligned.

3 Scoop the mold and deckle deeply into the pulp on the far edge of the bowl, and pull it toward you.

4 In one fluid motion, lift the mold and deckle cleanly away from the pulp. Keep it horizontal so that the pulp held within the frame does not tilt.

5 As soon as the mold and deckle is clear of the pulp, gently shake it from back to front and from left to right to help the pulp settle uniformly on the mesh. Stop as soon as the water has drained through the mesh.

6 Rest the frame on the side of the bowl while any excess water drains away. Alternatively drain it on a wad of newspaper.

7 Very carefully remove the deckle, making sure that you do not disturb the edges of the sheet. Avoid dripping water from the deckle onto the pulp, which could cause "holes" in the paper.

8 You can now see your sheet clearly formed with the characteristic, wavy, deckle edge of handmade paper. It is ready for immediate couching.

Use silver or soft brass wire (.030–.040 gauge) from a jewelry supply store, florist's wire, or any rustproof alternative. Bend this into the desired shape, and stitch it onto the top side of the screen on your mold. Snip off the loose ends of thread on the underside of the screen so that they will not affect the outline. When the wire is in place, form and couch your sheet.

Personalize your paper by creating individualized watermarks.

Couching

Once you have formed a sheet of wet pulp on the mold you will need to transfer it to a flat surface so that you can continue to use your mold and deckle to make additional sheets. This is known as couching. Before forming your sheet, prepare a couching board and a piece of felt or other absorbent material – a square of old blanket, a thick old towel, or an all-purpose kitchen cleaning cloth – to receive it.

1 Use a firm, varnished board 4 in. (10cm) wider than your sheet on all sides. Drill a hole at each corner to receive the bolts you will need later to press the paper (see p.130). Position damp felt over the board.

2 Rest one of the long edges of your mold along the board as shown.

3 Swiftly flip the mold over so that the pulp sheet is face down on the felt. Press down firmly on the sides of the mold.

4 Lift off the mold by raising the edge nearest to you and using a firm rolling action toward the opposite edge. This helps the sheet to adhere evenly.

5 The mold should come away cleanly, with little or no traces of pulp sticking to it. Place another piece of felt on top of the couched sheet and repeat the same process for other wet sheets.

Pressing

Once you have couched and layered the number of sheets you need, you must press them. This does two things: it squeezes out the excess water before drying and it helps to bond the fibers, so strengthening the sheet. Make your own press by adding a second wooden board to the pile of paper and felt and screwing it to the base board.

1 Place a varnished wooden board, identical to the base board, over the top felt sheet and screw it to your base board using 3 in. (7.5cm) bolts and wing nuts. Raise the press on two pieces of wood and leave it in a container.

2 After about 30 minutes, take the press from the container and remove the top board and felt. Carefully lift the next felt, with the sheet of paper on it, by diagonally opposite corners.

Drying

You can leave your sheet on the felt to dry, but this can be a slow process. Drying is quicker if you transfer the sheet to a smooth surface by upturning and removing the felt. If you find it difficult to turn your sheet out, place a piece of acetate over the top and turn over all three layers.

1 Place your sheet with the felt uppermost on a flat, clean, waterproof surface. Use a wide, soft brush to brush from the center to the outer edges of the felt. This will help the paper to adhere.

2 Carefully peel off the felt. Brush the paper to remove any loose surface fibers, and leave to dry overnight.

CREATING A RELIEF IMAGE

As an alternative to embossing a finished piece of paper (see p.40), you can create a relief image within the sheet as you are pressing it. One simple method is to use a waterproof stencil. Place it on the couched sheet and cover it with a piece of felt (or other absorbent material). To make sure that the stencil is pressed firmly into the pulp you will need to add several more layers of felt before you press and dry.

Subtle effects can be achieved with a relief image.

Embedding

There is endless scope for incorporating objects within a sheet of paper as you form it. Natural objects are especially suitable, but you can also create interesting effects with manufactured items, such as candy wrappers. The only criterion is that they be flat.

1 *Arrange the leaves on the mold. Once you have decided on their position, remove the leaves and mask the areas on which they will sit with masking tape.*

2 *Form and couch the paper. The pulp will only settle on the unmasked areas, forming four separate strips.*

3 *Place the leaves on the couched "sheet" in the positions you had chosen. Press the tips that overlap the pulp firmly to anchor them.*

4 *Remove the masking tape from the mold and form a second, entire, sheet of paper. Couch this directly on top of the original sheet, aligning the edges as closely as possible.*

5 *Allow the paper to dry. The second sheet will seal the leaves in place, but they will show clearly leaf side upward.*

Casting

You do not have to restrict yourself to making flat sheets of paper. You can make three-dimensional shapes using everyday objects such as this sieve as molds.

1 *Work with sheets that have been only lightly couched and so are still damp. Remove a triangular piece from the corner of a sheet by tearing against the blade of a blunt knife.*

2 *Lay the triangle into the mold. Add more triangles, overlapping the edges to create a seamless effect. Build up several layers in the same way, and leave to dry. Gently ease the cast from the sieve.*

Aromatic Paper

ART
FORMS

Handmade scented paper is both attractive to look at and delightful to smell. These sheets are ideal for using as notepaper for a special letter, or even for folding into envelopes. Sprinkle scented ingredients into your pulp for a textured, lightly perfumed effect, or blend scent into your pulp for a stronger fragrance. Your choice of scented ingredients is limitless, but be careful when using artificially dyed products, because they tend to bleed. Test for this by wetting the material. If the color runs, the dye is not fast, and it will leak into your paper. This is less important if you are pulping your ingredients, and indeed you may want to create the effect deliberately.

Incorporating natural objects •

Creating scented paper •

Combining color, texture, and scent •

These delicate, scented sheets will be treasured by the recipient of a letter written on them.

SCENTED PAPER

1 Select the dry ingredients that you want to include. If you are using flowers on stems, such as lavender, shake the flowerheads off and discard the stems.

2 After making a batch of pulp and coloring it (see pp.126–7) to match your scented ingredients, mix the pulp with water in the vat.

3 Sprinkle the lavender flowers evenly into the pulp.

4 Agitate the pulp with your hand to ensure that the flowers are mixed well.

5 Form, drain, and couch your sheet of paper. The texture will add visual interest to the delicate smell.

POTPOURRI PAPER

1 To make a more strongly perfumed sheet, use scented pulp. Liquify a potpourri of scented wood shavings in an electric blender three-quarters full of water.

2 Add the scented mixture to some colored pulp in the vat and mix well.

3 Form the sheet. The sheet will have a more regular surface than the lavender paper. Couch your sheet on top of the first lavender sheet.

Shaping Paper

ART FORMS

Once you have mastered the basics of forming and couching, you can adapt those techniques to create more un-usual pieces. Make your own irregularly shaped deckles, or utilize other craft frames, as we have done here. Masking areas on the mold gives further flexibility of shape.

Simple deckle shapes can be cut from ply-wood with a jigsaw. You can also use cookie cutters, cake molds, or a product called Buttercut (available from papermaking suppliers). If you are making stationery papers an envelope-shaped deckle is convenient. Experiment with hearts, stars,

Creating unusual shapes •

Masking areas on the mold •

Embedding objects within layers •

stars, animal shapes, festive figures such as Father Christmas, angels, and Christmas trees.

Here, three separate couched sheets were layered. There are two benefits to this technique: the varying thicknesses of the pulp over different areas gives a very pleasing effect; and if you want to use heavy items as embellishments, they can be anchored between the layers.

To preserve this fragile creation from dust and damage, it will need to be placed in a deep frame with a glass front.

1 To make a basic circular mold and deckle, stretch a piece of nylon curtain over a 12 in. (30 cm)-diameter embroidery frame. Tighten the outer ring and then trim off any excess nylon to the edge of the hoop.

2 Using a template, draw two semicircles on waterproof tape. Cut these out. Use the same template and a soft pencil to draw a circle on the center of the screen. Stick the tape in place using the pencil mark as a guide.

3 Use two or three different pulps. This will give an unusual effect to the finished piece. Add all the pulp to the vat and agitate well. A combination of half-stuff and pulp made from natural fibers was used here.

4 Form your sheet. You will notice that pulp will not adhere to the masked area, and so a hole will appear in the center of the sheet.

5 Couch the sheet. While it is still wet, apply lengths of string from the middle ring to the outside edge and beyond. As it becomes wet, the natural color of the string will be absorbed into the paper and leave a "printed" line.

6 Make a small circular sheet in the same way as the first one, using a 5½ in. (13.75cm) embroidery hoop mold. Mask the center. Laminate this sheet on top of the first one, trapping the string. Brush out with a soft brush.

7 Add feathers to the wheel, positioning them in such a way as to make a pleasing design with the string.

8 Form another circle of paper using the smaller mold, but do not mask the center. Place this solid circle over the center of the wheel, covering the base of the feathers. Take care when handling, as the circular sheet is fragile.

9 Use the soft brush to secure the feathers, and sponge off any excess water. You can now add decoration, such as knotting the ends of some of the strings or attaching tiny shells.

Cast Paper

Creating deep relief •

Constructing a mold •

Casting from a shape •

ART
FORMS

This cast paper piece was constructed using a simple shape. The geometric pattern is effective, but almost any shape can be made. The only guideline is that it should have sufficient depth to create a three-dimensional relief. If your cast shape is too shallow the effect will not be very different from that created by embossing a thick sheet. The deeper the relief, the greater the contrast between the two sides. Display whichever you prefer, or make two pieces from the same mold and present them as a pair, showing alternate sides.

The two sides of a mold look very different. Display whichever you prefer or make two pieces, perhaps using a contrasting color, from the same mold and display different sides.

1 *Construct a box 1½ in. (3.75cm) deep, using four strips of waterproof, varnished wood and a wooden or plastic-coated board for the base. The strips should be ½ in. (1.25cm) thick × 2 in. (5cm) deep and the board ½ in. (1.25cm) thick. The ends of the strips can overlap.*

2 *Screw the strips together with ¾ in. (1.8cm) screws. The strips should fit tightly around the base board but need not be screwed to it.*

3 *Seal all of the inner joints with silicone bathtub sealant, then turn the box over and seal the joints on the bottom. Leave to dry.*

4 *To make the cast, draw four long strips and two small triangles onto cardboard. Cut out the shapes and glue two of the strips together along their long edge, using waterproof adhesive tape. Angle the glued edge to form a raised "tunnel."*

5 *Glue the end triangles in place, and set aside to dry.*

6 *Pencil a line ¼ in. (6mm) from, and parallel to, the long edge of the third strip. Draw a row of triangles with this line as their base and cut them out, using a sharp blade against a straight edge, to form a serrated pattern. Repeat this method for the fourth strip.*

7 Apply waterproof tape to the uppermost surface of the cardboard tunnel and to one side of the serrated strips. Trim the pointed edges neatly to keep them sharp.

8 Glue the tunnel and serrated strips to the center of the casting frame as shown. Set aside.

9 Blend your pulp in an electric mixer, adding squares of soaked half-stuff in small batches.

10 Strain the pulp over a plastic container to remove the excess water. Transfer the pulp to a bowl.

11 Pour the strained pulp slowly over the shape in the frame. It will not pour smoothly and will tend to splash.

12 Once the bottom of the box is covered, start to firm the pulp down with your hands, making sure you remove any air bubbles.

13 *Sponge the surface of the pulp to soak up excess water. Keep the bowl into which you strained the pulp on hand, and squeeze out the sponge into it.*

14 *Build up the pulp over the higher areas of the shape by hand, pressing firmly to make sure the pulp adheres.*

15 *As a final check, feel for any thinner areas of pulp and add more if it seems necessary.*

16 *Sponge off any excess moisture, and allow to dry naturally in the frame. Drying time will depend on the thickness of the pulp and the surrounding temperature – it could take several days, or longer.*

17 *When the paper is dry, run a craft knife around the edge to break the silicone seal. Unscrew the frame.*

18 *Carefully slide a spatula under the corner of the paper in order to lift it from the baseboard.*

Papier mâché

Papier mâché is a medium that is versatile, inexpensive, and easily mastered. Its name is French for "chewed-up paper," referring to the two methods of making papier mâché: from roughly torn paper-strips or from a paper pulp. The first method is more common, because it uses basic household materials and needs no preparation. Papier mâché can be made into bowls, jewelry, wall ornaments, dolls, masks, and headdresses. It can also be a convincing substitute for traditional sculpture. Shape an armature of chicken wire to your chosen form, and layer it with papier mâché. Or cast your sculpture from a clay model or existing mold, such as a fruit or shell.

A papier mâché object is made by building up layers of glued paper strips on a mold or by using papier mâché pulp. When the layers are dry, the form is eased from the mold and decorated. Newspaper is a good material for papier mâché, because it is flexible when wet with glue. The layering and the paste give it strength, and its tendency to discolor – normally a disadvantage – does not matter because it will be painted. The newspaper must be torn, not cut, because the slightly irregular edges blend with less obvious seams when the strips are pasted down. To make objects from papier mâché you will need to make a mold. The easiest way of doing this is first to make a model from modeling clay, then to cast a mold in plaster of Paris. You will find it useful to acquire a couple of simple modeling tools. These come in a variety of sizes with wooden or wire ends and are useful for shaping the clay and separating the model from the mold.

When the form is released from the mold it can be trimmed and bound with additional torn paper. After preparing the surface with paint primer or gesso – a mixture of chalk, white pigment, and glue – you can then decorate your finished piece with poster colors or acrylic paint.

- ✓ Hand blender
- ✓ Paint brush
- ✓ Small scissors
- ✓ Craft knife
- ✓ Plastic buckets and bowls
- ✓ Rubber gloves
- ✓ Sieve
- ✓ Waterproof tape
- ✓ Modeling tools
- ✓ Polyvinyl acetate glue
- ✓ Wallpaper paste
- ✓ Vaseline
- ✓ Modeling clay
- ✓ Gesso
- ✓ Acrylic paints
- ✓ Varnish
- ✓ Plaster of Paris
- ✓ A variety of newspapers and waste paper torn into strips

LAYERED DECORATION

These colorful pots and dishes were decorated with paint and cut-out paper shapes. The artist layered the cut-outs directly on to the pots and sealed them under a coat of varnish.

CLAY MODEL CAST

The direct cast technique of laminated paper with white glue over a clay model was used to create this extremely ornate mask. Tissue paper was used for the final layer to give a good texture for painting and varnishing (George Bernard Shaw Mask, Billy Nicholas).

ARMATURE CAST

The sense of fun and attention to detail in this artist's work is created by his observation of the human figure and all its gestures. The method of construction is similar to the previous piece but here he builds up an armature of cardboard boxes covered with newspapers to create a life size character (The Hiker, Philip Cox).

WIRE FRAME CAST

This paper-only sculpture was constructed from paper pulp built onto a chicken wire frame, then painted and varnished (Louise Vergette).

Laminating

There are countless natural objects to cast from, such as shells, stones, bottles, bowls, or wall plaques. We have chosen a scallop shell, but whatever the item, the principle for casting is the same.

1 Rub a releasing agent, such as Vaseline, over the entire surface of the object. Do not leave any uncovered spots or the object may stick.

2 Tear some 1–1½ in. (2.5–3.75cm) wide strips of newspaper in the direction of the grain. You should have enough to cover the object. Then tear each strip into 1½ in. (3.75cm) lengths.

3 Mix some wallpaper paste in a bowl and immerse the paper strips so that each piece becomes thoroughly soaked.

4 Beginning at an edge, apply a strip of pasted paper and smooth it into place with your index finger. Add a second piece, overlapping the first by one third. Continue until you have covered the surface. Allow the paper to dry.

5 Tear some newsprint of a different color to form the following layer. Alternating colors helps you to keep track of the number of layers.

6 Apply the second layer in the same way as the first. Continue until you have eight layers, leaving the paper to dry between each application.

7 When the final layer is dry, trim the edges of the cast with scissors.

8 Pry the cast from the mold, easing it away from the edges until it comes free.

Reinforcing Edges

The newly made cast has a raw edge of paper layers that need to be reinforced to ensure that they do not come apart. This is achieved by applying one or two layers of pasted squares.

1 Tear some short strips of newspaper, a different color from your last layer. Paste them over the edge of the cast, from front to back, smoothing them with your finger.

2 Proceed all around the edge of the cast, overlapping each strip by one third. One or two layers is sufficient for an item of this size.

PREPARING FOR PAINTING

Papier mâché objects can be painted by brush, sponging, ragging, or spraying, but all methods need a white opaque base to give the colors vibrance. This is best achieved with gesso, which dries quickly and covers well, so you won't need multiple coats of paint to conceal the newsprint.

1 Apply gesso to the cast using a wide acrylic brush. Two coats should cover the newsprint and create a solid ground for your color.

2 Paint on acrylic color with the same brush. For a bright, uniform effect, apply the color with full intensity. If you want a more subtle wash, dilute the paint before applying. You can then remove color with a rag to leave just a hint behind.

3 Add texture by dipping a wrinkled paper towel or cotton rag into paint and dabbing it onto the cast. The painted surface takes on the imprint of the wrinkles.

Making Papier Mâché Pulp

Pulping is an alternative to layered papier mâché that can be pressed into a mold or formed by hand. Its advantage is that you can build up thickness quickly instead of waiting for each layer to dry. You can also impress patterns into the pulp.

1 *Tear 1 in. (2.5 cm) wide strips of newspaper with the grain, and tear again into 1–1½ in. (2.5–3.75 cm) lengths. Half fill a plastic pail.*

2 *Pour about 1 quart (1 liter) of water onto the paper. As the paper absorbs the water, it will sink considerably.*

3 *Mix the paper and water with your hand or a plastic spoon to distribute it evenly in the pail.*

4 *Use a hand blender to pulp the paper. Stab the blender into the mixture in short bursts so not to clog. Proceed until you have reduced all of the paper fibers to a slurry. Add water whenever the mixture seems too dry.*

5 *Pour the pulp through a sieve over a bowl to drain out the water.*

MAKING A SIMPLE MODELING CLAY MOLD

To construct your own creations from papier mâché you first need to make a mold. One of the simplest and most convenient materials to use is modeling clay. Whether you are shaping a simple relief mold like the one demonstrated here or a complex three-dimensional mold where paper is layered on all sides – as shown in the Mexican project (pp.150–1) – you will find this an ideal medium to sculpt.

1 *Draw your design on medium-weight paper and cut it out to create a template. Place it on a slab of rolled out modeling clay, and trace around the outside with a small wooden skewer.*

2 *Using a knife blade or wooden modeling tool, trim the excess clay from the scribed outline, then carve pieces away from areas that need thinning, such as the fish fins.*

Hand Pulping

Adding glue to pulp makes a modeling medium that sets hard and holds together well. You can use it on bowls, plaques, and ornaments, or over chicken wire armatures to make sculptures.

1 *Pour about 1 cup of polyvinyl acetate glue into a bowl of pulp. (Wallpaper paste can be used instead.)*

2 *Disperse the glue evenly throughout the bowl of pulp with your hands or a plastic spoon.*

3 *Coat your mold with a releasing agent, such as Vaseline, and press the pulp onto it. Apply a small amount at a time, pushing it firmly into place with your finger until you have covered the surface with a uniform layer.*

4 *You can add pulp to form a rim, pinching it tightly together and pressing it into the main pulp.*

5 *Create a pattern with a wooden modeling tool or with your fingers. The finished piece can then be removed from the mold, gessoed, and painted.*

3 *Trace out details from your template and trim them to the desired thickness. Attach them by overlapping them slightly and smoothing the joint with a wooden modeling tool.*

4 *When you are satisfied with the final shape of your mold, inscribe surface texture with various tools, or impress patterns using found objects.*

5 *Be careful not to create any sharp undercuts or over-projecting details that will prevent the release of the mold. Rub a releasing agent, such as Vaseline or liquid soap all over the mold.*

Pre-Columbian Mask

Building a clay model •

Making a plaster mold •

Casting with pulp •

ART
FORMS

This project is cast by hand pulping from a plaster mold (see p.143). Because pulp is applied to the inside of the mold, all of the features show on the outside of the cast, in contrast to over-layering techniques that keep the detail within. A model is first made in modeling clay (see pp.144–5). It is preferable to choose a simple shape without projections that may hinder removal of the cast from the mold.

Pulp can take several days to dry in a plaster mold, and undergoes some shrinkage. But when it is dry, the cast can be primed, decorated with various materials, and painted. A coat of varnish will seal it and allow cleaning with a damp cloth.

The plaque featured here is based on an image of Ehecatl, the Huastec god of the wind. The original is in the National Museum of Anthropology, Mexico City.

You could paint the mold terracotta, add gold polish, and then rub it back for an antique finish. Or, as we have here, paint the mold with a rich gold for an authentic Pre-Columbian effect.

1 *Use a plastic board for making your model. Complex images can be built up from simple rolled shapes. Use a modeling tool to incise details. Avoid tight corners or undercuts that could hinder removal from the mold.*

2 *Cut some strips of waterproof material at least ½ in. (1.25cm) higher than the model, and build a wall around it.*

3 *Fix the walls in place with waterproof tape so that plaster will not leak through, taking especial care to seal the corners.*

4 *You should rub Vaseline over the modeling clay. The Vaseline will act as a releasing agent.*

5 *Mix plaster of Paris to the manufacturers' instructions. A plastic bowl and spoon will be easiest to clean. Always wear gloves when working with plaster of Paris as it is an irritant to the skin.*

6 *As soon as the plaster is a smooth, creamy consistency, pour it over the clay model, filling to the top of the wall. Bang the work surface around the mold to bring air bubbles to the surface. Bubbles will form holes in the mold.*

7 *When the plaster is dry, remove the wall, and set the mold aside to cure. When the mold is cold and hard it is safe to remove the clay.*

8 *Carefully extract the clay from the mold, using a wooden pottery tool. Try to remove large pieces to avoid damaging fine detail in the mold.*

9 *Dig out remaining fragments with the tip of the pottery tool.*

10 *When the mold interior is completely clean, apply a light coating of Vaseline to the entire surface.*

11 *Tear enough squares of white paper to half-fill a small bucket. To add color, you can use watercolor paper. Add 5 cups of water and blend.*

12 *When the pulp is a smooth creamy consistency, strain it to remove excess water.*

13 *Transfer the pulp to a clean bowl. Add some wallpaper paste and mix well.*

14 *Take a handful of pulp and push it into the mold with your fingers. Make sure you press pulp firmly into all the detailed recesses as you fill the mold.*

15 *Continue pressing pulp into the mold until it is full, squeezing out any air pockets as you do so.*

16 *When the pulp has dried completely, remove the cast from the mold. Depending on the size of the cast, the pulp may take up to two weeks to dry out.*

17 *The pulp will shrink significantly as it dries. Trim off any loose pieces to neaten the outline.*

18 *Apply gesso or acrylic paint to seal the mold.*

Mexican Folk Art

Modeling a standing sculpture in clay •

Casting from a model by laminating •

ART FORMS

This project is cast by laminating, or building up layers of paper (see p.140). This technique produces a stronger, lighter cast than the papier mâché pulp method on pages 144–7, making it a more suitable technique for a free-standing figure such as this.

To make a free-standing figure like the Mexican folk art parrot, you will first have to make a model out of modeling clay (see pp.144–5). The cast is formed by layering paper over the model, cutting the cast in two, removing the clay, and rejoining the halves. This technique is popular because it is versatile, light, and inexpensive.

Our project has been painted. However, you can obtain interesting effects by using color comics, and then varnishing the finished cast to preserve the collage-like surface.

If you experiment with different types and strengths of paper you will find that layering offers a whole range of exciting possibilities.

Bright acrylic paints are in keeping with Mexican folk art and suit this project to perfection. This brilliantly colored bird would look wonderful on a themed Christmas tree, or in a child's room.

1 First shape the head and body. Next, form two wing shapes. Blend the clay together with a modeling tool. The bird was chosen for its simple shape; all you need is a basic form.

2 When you are happy with the form, add a few details such as the eyes and the strip over the head.

3 Rub a coating of Vaseline over the entire surface of the mold to ease its removal from the paper cast.

4 Tear two different-colored newspapers into manageable pieces that will conform to the mold details without wrinkling, and mix a medium-size bowl of wallpaper paste.

5 Cover the mold in a layer of paper squares, overlapping each piece and smoothing it thoroughly with your finger, so that all of the detail stands out. Leave to dry.

6 Apply a second layer, using the other color so that you can spot any missed or thin areas. Proceed in the same way until you have eight layers of paper.

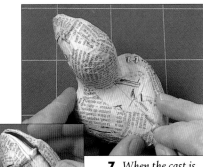

7 When the cast is completely dry, carefully cut around its center. Gently pry the halves apart and remove the mold.

8 Reunite the halves by pasting two contrastingly colored layers of newspaper squares along the joint.

9 When the parrot is dry, apply two coats of gesso to seal the cast.

Paper Sculpture

ART
FORMS

Sculpture can be made from virtually any paper. Recycled office paper, packaging, or junk mail, or choose from the standard and special papers carried by art supply stores. As you will see from the works in this book, extraordinary sculptures can be created in myriad colors and textures. However, the epitome of this art form is still considered to be white sculpture, with its graceful modeling of light and shade. Such classic pieces are often constructed from top-quality handmade watercolor papers whose high cotton rag content gives strength and malleability.

Unlike traditional sculpture materials, paper cannot be shaped into a compound curve, that is, a form that curves in two directions. When the second curve is made, the first curve springs back. However, you can create a similar effect by gluing two pieces of paper together. Most of the other restrictions inherent in paper can be overcome by careful cutting, curling, scoring, and shaping.

Mastering the following techniques is crucial to success in this art form. Practice them thoroughly as a sound basis for your own creativity.

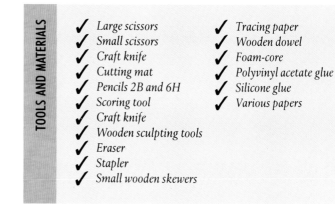

TOOLS AND MATERIALS

- ✓ Large scissors
- ✓ Small scissors
- ✓ Craft knife
- ✓ Cutting mat
- ✓ Pencils 2B and 6H
- ✓ Scoring tool
- ✓ Craft knife
- ✓ Wooden sculpting tools
- ✓ Eraser
- ✓ Stapler
- ✓ Small wooden skewers
- ✓ Tracing paper
- ✓ Wooden dowel
- ✓ Foam-core
- ✓ Polyvinyl acetate glue
- ✓ Silicone glue
- ✓ Various papers

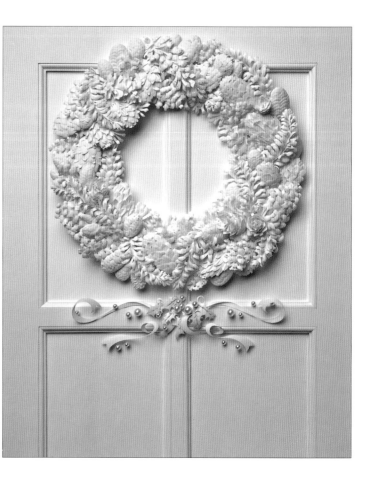

SHADOW AND HIGHLIGHTS
*This delicate, all-white sculpture captures the elegance of paper sculpture in its purest form. Here the shapes are given life by the way each piece interacts with light and shade (*White Wreath, *Joanna Bandle).*

COLOR ENHANCEMENTS

To create this sculpture the artist used colored papers and then embellished some pieces further by adding painted color to create a graduated tone, or a spattered background. These techniques further enhance a composition, giving an added illusion of depth in areas that may not be naturally modeled by light (Sally Jo Vitsky).

TEXTURED PAPER

A subject that is popular in any illustrative medium is the cat (above). Here simple, graphic shapes are given more interest by the use of fur texture embossed paper (Rousseau's Cat, Clive Stevens).

THREE-DIMENSIONS

To create a three-dimensional effect the artist has cut and curled printing papers and then added texture with pastels. The frame becomes part of the composition (Wood duck, Bill Finewood).

Basic Shapes

Most paper sculpture shapes are created by cutting, scoring, folding and curling. Using combinations of the basic shapes demonstrated here, you will be able to construct more complex pieces.

Scored lines are indicated on the diagrams by dotted lines. When scoring, it is best to bend paper away from the scored line. When scoring alternating valley and mountain folds (see p.53) you will need to turn the paper over to score the correct side.

U SHAPE

Cut out a large letter U and score a valley fold in the middle with a mountain fold either side. Pull one side of the U over the other and glue in position.

ZIG-ZAGS

On a rectangular shaped piece of paper, score five vertical marks, then score eight zig-zag horizontal lines with alternating valley and mountain folds.

SCORED CONE

Cut out a circle and score four circular lines, as shown, to create alternating valley and mountain folds. Cut out a segment, pull the edges together and glue.

CONE

Cut out a circle and remove a quarter segment, then bring the ends together to form a cone and glue.

TIPS FOR PAPER SCULPTING

✓ *Work methodically from background to foreground so that each piece you add hides the gluing points of the previous piece.*

✓ *Paint the paper components before you sculpt them since water-based paints tend to flatten sculpted shapes.*

✓ *Keep your hands clean and free of pastel dust. Dirty finger marks will ruin a sculpture.*

✓ *Avoid water-based glues when working with thin paper. They will soak in and leave wrinkles. Use a clear household adhesive.*

✓ *When raising paper components with blocking, make sure that it remains neat and carefully hidden.*

✓ *When using polyvinyl acetate glue, keep it in a small flexible plastic container lid. This will bend and allow you to remove hardened glue easily.*

✓ *If you decide to make a limited edition of a particular image, cut out all the pieces and then use them as templates to trace out identical pieces for the edition. Be sure to label all your templates clearly.*

✓ *When working on an all-white sculpture, it is helpful to place a desk lamp in the position of the final light source. In this way, you can gauge the effect of the light on each piece as you add it to the sculpture.*

WAVY LINES

Cut out a rectangle with top and bottom edges as wavy lines. Score six horizontal wavy lines with alternating valley and mountain folds.

SWEEPING CURVE

On a rectangular shaped piece of paper score a curve from side to side to create a valley fold. Then score a corresponding curve on either side to create two mountain folds.

STAR

Cut out a five-pointed star. From the center to each point, score a mountain fold. From the center to the joint between each point score a valley fold.

FOUR FOLD

On a square piece of paper, score a series of equidistant horizontal lines for alternating valley and mountain folds. This is also called a fan fold.

TRIANGLE

Draw four joining triangles, as shown, and score the dividing line between each. Fold along the scored lines and glue the fourth triangle behind the first.

CUBE

Draw the six squares, as shown, with glue tabs attached to them. Cut out and score all the joining lines and tabs. Fold together and glue tabs to attach.

CYLINDER

Take a rectangular piece of paper and curl over the edge of a table to form a tube. Open up and glue one edge. Bring the other end over to attach them together.

LEAF

Cut out a leaf shape and score an S-shaped line along the central axis. Fold back to create a mountain fold.

Special lighting

Lighting plays a key role in modeling the elements of your sculpture, especially if it is all-white. This is important not only when planning and displaying your work, but when photographing it. Professionals use tungsten lamps, sometimes with colored gels that bathe a white sculpture in tinted light. But you can achieve good results by photographing your sculpture in natural light. Choose a bright day but avoid brilliant sun, since this causes dark shadows. If one side is too dark, position a piece of white cardboard near it but out of camera shot to reflect light into the work.

However you light your work, it always looks best using only one light source. Experiment to find the situation and angle that suits each piece. The aim is to make the image appear to jump off the paper and to do justice to the originality of your work.

LIGHTING WHITE SCULPTURE

When photographing white sculpture, remember that since you do not have color to define the form, your results rely purely on light and shade to model every detail. Therefore the positioning of the light source is vital.

STRONG LIGHT – FLAT MOUNT

The lighting of the bee is not too far astray, but the piece lacks impact due to the mount being flat against the background.

FLAT LIGHT – RAISED MOUNT

Here the mount is raised but the light is too flat, creating an insipid look that fails to reflect the original.

Good strong light gives an even overall color.

Shadows under the wings are nicely diffused but give a convincing feeling of three-dimensionality.

Raising the mount off the background creates shadows that increase the 3-D quality.

The ribbed body is well defined with subtle shadows, as is the honeycomb background.

SIDE LIGHT – FLAT MOUNT

The detail of the bee's body stands out under this lighting, but the effect is harsh and unpleasing.

SIDE LIGHT – RAISED MOUNT

This shot was constructed to show maximum modeling when lit. The result, however, is unbalanced; some parts of the modeling are sharp, while others are less distinct. The mount is flat and lacking in detail.

CREATING TEXTURE IN PAPER

PILLARS

Score a series of vertical lines ⅛ in. (3mm) apart by running a metal stylus along a ruler. Turn the paper over and roll it into a tube with ribs like those of a pillar.

SWIRLS

Place a sheet of paper on top of a piece of foamcore board. Press shapes into it with a metal stylus. This is a good method for creating the textures of foliage.

STONES

Place some foam rubber in a flower press, and sprinkle small pebbles onto it as shown. Cover with a sheet of dampened paper and another piece of foam. Screw the press down securely, and leave for a day or two until the paper is dry. Remove the sheet. It will be textured with the imprint of the stones.

Adding Dimension

Raising components creates shadow and dimension, and results in a more interesting composition. Most relief paper sculptures use this method. Glue matchsticks, corrugated cardboard or a small block of foamcore board to the underside. Foamcore comes in ¼ in. (6mm) and ⅛ in. (3mm) thicknesses. If you want a greater depth, sandwich several layers with glue.

USING MATCHSTICKS

1 *To raise small components, use a craft knife to cut matchsticks to length.*

2 *Glue the matchsticks to the back of the shape.*

BLOCKING SHAPES

3 *For larger components, apply foamcore board in the same way to provide a strong, light support. Corrugated cardboard would also be suitable.*

4 *The resulting shape stands out from the surface, casting a natural shadow that gives the composition a wonderful sense of depth.*

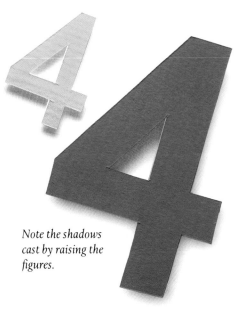

Note the shadows cast by raising the figures.

GLUING POINTS

When assembling paper sculptures, it is important to consider all the elements of the construction, not just the parts visible in the finished piece.

1 *If you cut out this penciled image exactly, you will not have sufficient overlap to glue the leaves together. You must therefore extend the leaf that sits underneath to make it the gluing point for the other leaves.*

2 *Place a dab of glue on the single leaf and attach it to the back of the double leaf. Press for a few seconds between your finger and thumb until the adhesive sets.*

Making an Armature

Three-dimensional objects often need an armature to support them. This can be made from cardboard, wooden dowels, or chicken wire molded to the shape of your sculpture (especially useful for paper mâché).

1 *Curl a rectangle of paper over the edge of a table. Press it with one hand while pulling the paper sheet down with the other hand.*

2 *Roll the curled paper into a tube, and staple the ends in place.*

3 *Repeat to create a smaller tube, but this time glue it together because a stapler will not fit.*

4 *Hold the small tube in position across the larger tube, and cut it to length with scissors.*

5 *With a sharp knife make an incision in the larger tube where the crosspiece is to be inserted. Do this in both sides of the tube. Make sure your fingers are safely out of the way.*

6 *Push the smaller tube into place through the incisions.*

7 *The tube opens the cuts just enough to pass through, and will therefore be held tightly.*

8 *You can now apply the component that needs support.*

Fashion Model

ART FORMS

Creating a fully rounded sculpture •

Working with basic shapes •

Constructing the human figure •

When building a free-standing sculpture, think of each component as a basic geometric form: a cube, a cylinder, or a cone. Most shapes can be derived from these. A human body can be created from a cube with tapered sides, a head from a cylinder with facial features, and arms and legs from tapered cylinders. However, sculpture "in the round" is considered difficult because you cannot rely on a single perspective sketch of your subject. You must consider the back and sides of each cut-out element, and where to add gluing tabs. Keep your shapes simple and within the limitations of the medium. Remember to allow for the spread of your sculpture, that is, the entire wraparound area. The shape of a head mask, for example, that will look normal when curled around from ear to ear, appears unnaturally wide when flattened out.

Use paper that is sturdy enough to support the sculpture: the larger the sculpture, the

heavier the paper. Keep your scoring neat – a messy line can mar the finished effect – and avoid halfway creases when curling and shaping. Gluing is easier if you clamp pieces with rubber bands and paper clips until set. With a little practice you will begin to construct complicated shapes.

The shades of mauve and purple enhance the sophisticated appearance of this paper sculpture. The colors of your sculpture should always be chosen with the final effect in mind.

TEMPLATES

Make an enlarged photocopy of the templates to the size you require and trace each one onto a sheet of medium-weight tracing paper with a 2B pencil. Remember that continuous lines indicate cut lines, and dotted lines show lines to be scored.

Start by sketching your sculpture. From this draw your templates, isolating manageable sections of the figure.

body

neck

flower

earing

bow tie

lapels

hat

nose

face

lips

hair

blouse

glove

hat

sleeve

neck

161

1 Cut out the main body piece. Cut through all the continuous lines with a sharp blade, and use a metal stylus to score the broken lines.

2 Fold all the tabs along the scored lines and then flatten the folds with your thumb.

3 To create a neat centerfold for the shoulder, place a ruler along each shoulder line and fold up against it.

4 Fold the body into its finished shape and check that everything fits snugly before gluing.

5 Glue the two pleats in the front of the chest and adhere to the gluing lines. Paste the shoulder tabs in position.

6 Glue the side tabs together, and attach as shown.

7 Complete the body by pasting and adhering the small tabs at the top of the arm position.

8 To make the neck, take a tapered rectangle of pale flesh colored paper and curl it over the edge of a table. Roll the sheet into a tapered tube and staple at the bottom only. This will allow the top to be adjusted if necessary.

9 Insert the narrow end of the tube through the neck hole and glue into position. Adjust the diameter of the tube to fill the opening and staple it.

10 *Cut out the two flesh colored head pieces, incising the slits for cheeks, mouth, and nose. Score and shape the two lines on either cheek.*

11 *Curl both the head pieces over the table edge as before.*

12 *Using a thin wooden dowel, curl the ears forward slightly. Check their position from the front and adjust.*

13 *Cut out the nose and score down the center to form a mountain fold with a valley fold on either side to serve as fixing tabs. Insert the nose into the head slots and glue from the back.*

14 *Glue the other head piece together. This will act as the foundation for the main head piece.*

15 *Staple the main head piece to its foundation by the tabs at either side of the head as shown.*

16 *Cut out the hair and curl it around the back of the head. Connect the slits over the ears and staple into position.*

17 *Cut out the hat parts, and score and fold the hat strip. Make a series of cuts ⅛ in. (3mm) apart along the fold edge on either side of the strip.*

18 *Curl the strip into a cylinder and insert it through the brim. Adjust the diameter to fit, and glue into position.*

19 *Fold back the glue tabs and attach them to the brim.*

20 *Fold down all of the tabs on the crown of the hat and glue the top disk over them. Turn the hat upside down and firm the tabs into position.*

21 *Cut out, curl, and attach the hatband, gluing the joint at the back.*

22 *Cut out and shape the flower, using four scored lines: two on one side and two on the reverse.*

23 *Place the hat on the head. There is no need to glue it if it fits snugly.*

24 *Paste the back of the flower, and fix it to the hatband. Dot the middle with glue and add the purple center.*

25 *Cut out the lips and score along the center. Fold back slightly and glue to the mouth slit.*

26 *Glue the blouse front to the jacket. Curl the collar around the neck and glue at the back.*

27 *Adhere one side of the lapels to the bottom of the blouse. Curl the lapel around the neck, then glue the end over the first point at the bottom.*

28 *Cut out arm pieces, curl, and glue into tapered cylinders. Round the top of the arms with scissors, put some glue inside, and pinch together to adhere.*

29 *Cut the left arm to length, glue at the top, and fix to the side of the body.*

30 *Glue inside the back of the head, and position it on the neck so that the chin protrudes.*

31 *Cut a V from the middle of the right arm to create an elbow joint. Cut out the mauve glove.*

32 *Glue the inside of the V cut in the upper arm, then bend the lower arm up and hold in position until the glue sets. Cut the hand over a dowel.*

33 *Glue the right arm to the body, holding it firmly so that it remains flat.*

34 *Glue the hand to the wrist, then carefully curl the fingers over and adhere them to the hat brim.*

35 *Assemble the earrings, glue at the back, and secure to the ears.*

36 *Put together the bow tie, glue the neck of the blouse, and attach.*

Bird in Flight

ART FORMS

Relief sculpture achieves its illusion of depth by using shapes cut out in perspective and elaborated at varying levels to create a natural shadow when the work is lit. This method has become popular in modern advertising and book illustration as an alternative to painting or drawing. Some contemporary paper sculptors will use only white paper to create the classic works that capture the essence of the medium and rely on light and shade to model their graceful lines. Others exploit the full range of colored and textured papers, or use recycled materials, such as corrugated cardboard, newspapers, paper towels, and cardboard tubes. Your choice is virtually unlimited. If a flimsy paper would achieve a particular effect but is too light to shape, laminate it to a heavier material, such as watercolor paper — remnants of this are sometimes available in art supply stores.

Foamcore board is one of the most convenient methods for elevating components, because it is light, easy to cut and glue, and holds its shape well. Mount your completed sculpture on a backing board and frame it to last for years.

• Creating a relief sculpture
• Scoring and curling in sculpture
• Constructing a sculpture over a drawing

The finished sculpture can be mounted on a backing board and then framed.

WORKING DRAWING AND TEMPLATES

Make an enlarged photocopy of these templates and the working drawing to the size you require. Mark the color for each piece on your photocopied set.

Beak

Eye

H1

B1

B2

B3

W7

W8

W9

H1

W18

W10

W16

W11

H2

W12

W13

W14

W14

W13

B1

W6

W12

W15

W6

T1

W5

T2

W17

W5

W4

W3

W10

W1

W2

W1

W7

W8

W9

W2

W3

W11

W4

KEY
Tail (T)
Wing (W)
Body (B)
Head (H)
↔ Grain line

W15

W16

W18

W17

T2

T1

USING A WORKING DIAGRAM

When creating a complex sculpture with a large number of small pieces, it is essential to use your working drawing as a positional guide. Once you have cut and shaped the pieces, place your drawing flat on the table and begin to build up the bird, matching each piece to the tracing.

BIRD IN FLIGHT

1 *Trace the diagram from an enlarged photocopy, and mark the colors.*

2 *Turn the tracing face down on a sheet of blue paper, and trace the outline of the wings with a hard pencil. Make sure you follow the grain of the paper and you leave enough overlap for the back wing to hide under the body (see template).*

3 *Trace all of the blue parts. Cut them out and put them aside.*

4 *Cut the main body slit as indicated on the template. This is the connecting slit that fits around the bird's neck.*

5 *Curl the main blue body part over the edge of a table two or three times to ensure an even curve.*

6 *The smaller pieces are easier to curl around a dowel.*

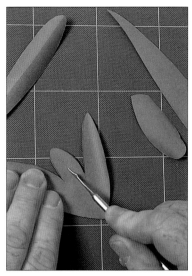

7 Cut and shape the red head piece, then the gray wing parts. Curl each feather in the wing piece over the dowel individually.

8 Cut the remaining gray pieces, and curl each one lengthwise.

9 Take the gray tailpiece and score a central line along each feather. Bend the lines back to form a mountain fold.

10 Repeat this scoring and folding process on the wing feathers.

11 Cut and shape the white breast and body pieces. Glue the top straight edge only and adhere to the white body. Note how the bird is built up using the tracing as a guide.

12 Cut and shape the black eye piece. Glue the top edge as shown, and attach the blue head piece to it.

13 *Secure the blue cap with eye to the red head piece. Apply a strip of glue around the top edge only, so that the head does not sit too flat.*

14 *Assemble the beak parts and attach to the underside of the head as shown.*

15 *Taking the main body part in one hand, and the head in the other, slide the two pieces together, ensuring that the tabs interlock as shown.*

16 *Turn the assembly over and glue the back of the red tab. Hold in position for a few seconds to adhere.*

17 *Glue the top straight edge of the white body part and attach the blue body and head, smoothing the glued area with your thumb.*

18 *Cut out a tiny white oval, and glue it to the top of the eye to indicate the reflection of light.*

19 *Glue the top edge of the gray back wing feathers and secure the blue front feathers to it.*

20 *Glue the end of each gray primary feather in turn and attach to the underside of the wing assembly. Use your tracing as a position guide.*

21 *Glue the two feathered tail parts on top of the three feathered pieces. Slide the assembled tail between the blue and white body parts, and glue the tail into place.*

22 *Cut some tapered lengths of ¼ in. (6mm) foamcore board to act as blocking for the wings.*

23 *Glue a 1 in. (2.5cm) x ½ in. (1.25cm) block of foamcore to the underside of the front wing. Then glue the other side of the block and attach it to the body.*

24 *Glue a similar foam block to the front of the back wing and attach the wing to the body.*

Storage and Display

When you have completed your work you may want to display it. Flat pieces of art can be framed in the conventional way, but many pieces will be three dimensional, and so present a greater challenge.

Works that are designed to be viewed from one side only can be displayed in a deep shadow box frame. You can buy these ready-made at a framing store, but the depth of the molding is usually no more than 1½ in. (3.8cm), so you may have difficulty with bulkier pieces. You can have your work professionally framed to fit, or you can make your own, following the instructions given for the Menagerie Sampler on pages 48 to 49.

Larger pieces, or pieces designed to be viewed from all sides, such as sculptures, should be placed on flat surfaces. You may even want to use a turntable of some sort to facilitate easy viewing. Paper is a delicate medium, so if you are concerned about dust or moisture damaging your work, you may prefer to protect it in a glass display case. Remember that good lighting is paramount – for advice on how to light your work, see page 158.

Deciding whether to buy a clip-on frame or something more elaborate depends on your budget.

You can make minor repairs to your work if the paper becomes torn or if your papier mâché and paper sculpture creations get squashed or dented:

- *For tears, apply a thin layer of glue to a small strip of medium-weight cardboard. Slide the cardboard between the tear to transfer the glue and remove. Carefully press the torn pieces together or burnish down with a roller.*

- *To reinforce weak points caused by folds or thin areas from the papermaking process, paste a piece of thin paper, such as tissue or thin bond, to the back of the damaged paper.*
- *To repair dents, insert a dowel or knitting needle inside the piece and carefully push the dent outward.*

You may not want to keep your art on permanent display. Even if you are less than happy with the results, do not discard any project. The versatile nature of Paper Craft lends itself to recycling, and so you may be able to incorporate your early attempts into future projects. At the very least, they will prove useful for reference.

A flat file is ideal for storing large pieces of flat work.

Flat pieces can be stored in a folder and put in a filing cabinet or flat file.

Any work that is not flat should be wrapped carefully and placed in a box.

Index

Credits

Quarto would like to thank all the artists who kindly allowed us to publish their work in this book, including the following who provided demonstrations: Edwin Corrie, Sophie Dawson, Jennifer James, Paul Jackson.

We would like to thank Specialist Crafts Ltd., Leicester for loaning a mold and deckle for photography, Robert Cunning for making the frame on pages 48-9, and Dorothy Frame for the index.

We would also like to acknowledge the following owners of featured work (key: a = above; b = below): John Frost Historical Newspaper Service 8a; Whatmans plc 8b; The Japanese Gallery, London 9a; ET Archive 10b.

All project photographs are the copyright of Quarto plc.